TWO WORDS I'D NEVER SAY AGAIN

A SWEET ROMANTIC COMEDY

REMI CARRINGTON

Copyright ©2020 Pamela Humphrey
All Rights Reserved
Phrey Press
www.phreypress.com
www.remicarrington.com
First Edition

This is a work of fiction. Names, characters, businesses, places, events, and incidents are either the products of the author's imagination or used in a fictitious manner. Any resemblance to actual persons, living or dead, or actual events is purely coincidental.

All rights reserved. This book or any portion thereof may not be reproduced or used in any manner whatsoever without the express written permission of the publisher except for the use of brief quotations in a book review.

ISBN-13: 978-1-947685-50-5

❀ Created with Vellum

CHAPTER 1

*J*ust because I didn't want to be the one standing in front of a crowd and promising forever to someone—once was enough for me—didn't mean I couldn't be happy for my business partner and former sister-in-law. The word former was questionable, but that wasn't something I was prepared to discuss with anyone . . . especially my ex, who at the moment was sitting right beside me at the rehearsal dinner, repeatedly tapping his name card on the table.

Was I bitter? A little.

Deeply hurt? Blindingly so.

None of that made this weekend any easier.

A woman with wild, copper curls walked up to the table. "Hank Sparks, introduce me to your bride. I am so sorry I missed your wedding. Has it really been eighteen months since then?"

Hank turned the color of a freshly power-washed sidewalk. "Aunt Joji, hi. This is Nacha."

That was it? He wasn't going to say anything else? No mention of the fact that our happily-ever-after imploded months after the wedding when Hank moved to a different state?

Doing my best to hide the uncomfortable thumping on the inside of my skull, I smiled. "I've heard so much about you." 'So much' translated to snippets of stories about a very wealthy but a somewhat eccentric, aunt.

She wrapped me in a hug, and the sleeve of her flowy muumuu landed in Hank's drink. "I like you. People with interesting names should stick together. And I'm so sorry about the confusion with your room. They should've had it ready for you."

"It's fine. I used Haley's room to get ready."

Aunt Joji tapped her sides, then stuck a hand in her pocket. "Here they are." She handed me a keycard and then to my horror, handed one to Hank. "They bumped y'all up to one of the nicer cabins. And I added an extra night. Enjoy!" Waving, she floated through the room.

I grabbed the table and counted to ten . . . then twenty. How high did I have to count before the urge to strangle Hank dissipated? "She thinks we're still married."

Hank rubbed his chin. "I haven't seen her in ages. And with everyone so happy about the wedding, I didn't bring it up."

I finished my drink, contemplating a second. "Fix it. I don't care what you have to do. Fix it."

"I will." He sighed. Just as the waiter started serving dinner, Hank left the table. "I'll do it right now."

I picked at my salad. Would anyone notice if I crumbled a chocolate bar on top? If I broke it into small enough pieces, maybe they would assume my salad had cacao nibs on it. Alcohol hadn't been part of my plan for the weekend, but I had twelve bars of dark chocolate in my bag. And one in my purse.

Remembering to smile, I counted to three as I breathed

in, then after holding my breath for a second, I let it out slowly. Coming to this wedding required every ounce of courage I had. Embarrassed, I was prepared to face questions about my failed marriage. Nothing had prepared me to pretend like I was happily married.

Hank walked back across the room. The tiny part of me that didn't ache with every breath, that part missed being married to him.

Without looking at me, he dropped back into his chair and downed his drink, the one the sleeve had tainted. He wasn't about to share good news. "They're full."

"What about the room I was supposed to have?" I rubbed my temples, then dropped my hands into my lap.

His voice rumbled with emotion. "Believe me, I asked. *Nothing* is available. Someone booked the last few rooms a few minutes ago. Just be thankful we have a suite."

Great. For the entire wedding weekend, I'd be sharing a suite with Hank.

He glanced at his bowl. "We should probably eat."

"Probably. Want some chocolate?"

"They don't have any of the good kinds in the little shop in the lobby. I checked. I figured you'd want some since . . . you're stuck with me." He picked up his fork. "Sorry about that."

"I brought my own."

"Of course you did. Because you knew I'd be here."

"Your sister is getting married. Of course you'd be here." I finally tasted the salad. "Wow, this is good. You should try it."

He picked up his fork. "I really am sorry."

I'd heard too many of his apologies.

We survived dinner. The lack of conversation could be blamed for why we finished our food before any other table. Watching Zach and Haley flirt over dinner proved an entertaining distraction. Focused on them, I acted like I didn't notice Hank studying me.

After dinner, the guests moved out of the private dining room onto the back patio. Just when I thought the rehearsal dinner was over, phase two was just getting started. My smile needed to last a little longer.

Being included in the wedding party meant enjoying an entire wedding weekend, not just a few hours on a Saturday.

I was doing this for Haley.

Putting on my best smile, I joined the others outside.

Hank mumbled an apology, then walked away.

After having drinks with dinner—I'd only had one—guests were relaxed. I didn't do relaxing well, so fitting in now would be a chore.

Cocktail tables surrounded a pool, and on the lawn, a game of Cornhole was waiting to be played. Firelight from bamboo torches lit the area, and portable heaters chased away the chill in the November air.

Most of the guests wandered toward the game, ready to toss the beanbags. A few made their way to benches out on the lawn to watch the competition. But I found a spot at a cocktail table, close enough to the other guests to be polite but far away enough to enjoy a moment alone.

All I needed now was another cocktail. Wind gusted, and I fought to keep my dress down. Pale yellow and flowy, it wasn't suited for windy situations. All the advice about wearing pretty undergarments to improve self-confidence didn't take into account wind.

I glanced around, making sure I hadn't unintentionally given anyone a peep show. Hank's gaze snapped away. Why did it hurt to catch him staring? It had been more than a year. Why couldn't I move on?

His shoulders tensed as he tried his level best not to look at me. While he watched Cornhole like it was an Olympic sport, I took the opportunity to admire how good he looked. During dinner, I couldn't stare without him noticing. He'd lost a bit of weight, and the extra muscles in his arms suited him. The usual stubble was gone. Clean-shaven cheeks coordinated better with dress shirts and tuxes, his attire for the weekend.

Cheers sounded from the guests gathered around the game. Haley threw her arms in the air. It was good to see her getting her happily-ever-after, but it shaded my vision with a tint of green. I snuck another look at Hank.

I knew I'd be seeing him this weekend. I'd mentally prepared myself, but I'd done a shoddy job. How would I share a room with him all weekend? And why hadn't he mentioned to his extended family that we hadn't been happily married in over a year? Learning we were sharing a room almost undid me, but I'd maintained my control.

My smile never faded.

My life in its current state was all about maintaining my walls. I'd become quite skilled in keeping up a good front.

Haley's Aunt Joji sashayed toward my table, her muumuu blowing in the breeze. "Nacha, I do hope we can get to know each other better. Since I've been traveling for the last two years, I've missed so much. But just seeing the way Hank looks at you, I can see how happy you are." Perhaps she needed glasses. "Tell me about your name."

My gaze cut to Hank. When he winked, I pressed the heel of my shoe into my other foot. He was a lot like my very expensive heels. They looked great but hurt so much.

Aunt Joji cleared her throat, and I turned back to the table, frustrated with myself for staring at Hank.

"My given name is Ignacia, but everyone calls me Nacha. It's easier to say."

"I get that. Georgia Jean is what my mama called me

when I was in trouble. Other than that, everyone called me Joji."

A young man approached, a drink in his hand and a wide smile on his face. "Hi! Zach says I should call you Aunt Joji."

She tucked an arm around his waist. "Absolutely. Are you having a good time?"

"I am. It was kind of you to invite me tonight." His green eyes danced with excitement.

"We couldn't have Zach's cousin missing all the fun. I am sorry you have to work tomorrow." She patted the table. "Join us. I'm hoping the waiter will find me. I wasn't anywhere near here when I ordered my drink."

He stepped up to the table next to me, and I inched over, wary of the pool behind me.

Grinning, he stuck out his hand. "Eli Gallagher."

The Gallagher family resemblance was hard to miss.

"Nacha." Leaving off my last name saved lots of questions.

Aunt Joji lit up like the night sky on the Fourth of July. "This is Hank's wife. You know him, right?"

"I sure do. So nice to meet you." He rubbed the back of his head. "But I thought . . . never mind." He lifted his beer bottle and used it to point. "Haley is pretty good at that game."

"She practices a lot so she can beat Hank." I clenched the fabric of my skirt, trying to keep it from flying up.

Zach pointed at our table. "Eli, get over here."

"She'll probably beat me too." Eli chuckled, then walked away.

Aunt Joji patted my hand. "Everyone seems to be having a great time."

"It was so nice of you to treat Haley and Zach to all this." I shifted farther away from the pool.

Water and I did not get along. When I was seven, I'd fallen in a pool and nearly drowned. I hadn't been in one since.

A waiter walked up with two drinks on his tray. "Ladies, these are for you."

"You found me! What a dear." Aunt Joji pressed a hand to her heart.

If I'd only heard her talk and had someone describe her clothing, I would have expected Aunt Joji to be a large woman. She wasn't. Not even five feet tall, she was thin as a twig.

"A mojito for you, as requested." He handed her a glass. "And from the gentleman, this is for you." The waiter set a glass on the table in front of me.

This time when I glanced up, Hank met my gaze. He was better at faking happily married than living it.

I smiled and gave a small nod.

When he'd gotten me a drink before dinner, I'd discovered a new favorite. But no matter how good the mix of Coke, vanilla syrup, and vodka tasted, I would not allow myself too many. That would only get me into trouble. I didn't need my defenses down when Hank and I would be sharing a suite.

"After booking this place, it struck me how it probably seems like I'm playing favorites since I wasn't around for your wedding. I assure you, I love both these kids—well, they aren't kids anymore. And I'm not playing favorites. I just haven't had a chance to talk to you and Hank about my plan. I'd never want anyone to think I loved one more than the other. I've booked that little romantic cabin over there"—she pointed to a cheerily lit cabin down a path—"for an extra night for y'all to enjoy. Even after a year, I can see y'all are still in that wonderful honeymoon phase. And, speaking of honeymoons . . ." She turned as Zach laughed and spun Haley around.

No one was talking about honeymoons except Aunt Joji.

Hank and I weren't even next to each other. How was she dreaming up the image of a gushy, starry-eyed couple?

She sighed as she sipped her mojito. "I just love these. But too many, and I'll fall in that pool. *That* would be embarrassing." Ice clinked in the glass as she shook it. "But one more won't hurt. Now what was I saying? Oh! I'm sending y'all on a second honeymoon."

I couldn't continue pretending Hank and I were still a couple. "Aunt Joji—"

"No buts. This is important to me." Georgia Jean Sparks was a force to be reckoned with.

"Thank you." I stared at the cabin. A pebble-stone path led away from the patio in that direction. I lifted my glass, thankful for the drink. It tasted good and gave me something to do.

"Secluded. That's why I booked it for you two."

I choked, and Coke splattered down the front of my dress.

"Oh no. Your dress!" In her haste to wipe at the pale-yellow fabric, Aunt Joji bumped the glass, launching the rest of my drink at me. Coke covered my dress, and the glass shattered on the ground, drawing attention from everyone at the party.

"My dear. I am so sorry."

"It's fine. I'll be fine." I tried to decide on the quickest escape. "I'm just going to slip into the ladies' room."

"But you'll come back, right? It's much too early to hide in your room."

"Of course." There went my plan of ducking out early.

The waiter arrived with a broom.

Embarrassment probably had my cheeks colored an awful shade of red. "I'm so sorry."

He winked. "No problem. It happens more than you think."

Aunt Joji waved at Haley. "I should mix and mingle. I'll see you again in a bit. I am sorry."

"Don't worry about it." I walked to the bathroom in the lobby. Wetting paper towels, I dabbed at the spots.

They faded a little, but wetting the fabric made the dress completely see-through. I turned on the hand dryer and prayed no one would walk in. Contorted, I positioned myself under the blower, hoping to dry my dress a little. I was probably just setting the stains with the heat and giving myself hot flashes.

Why had I worn this dress? It only reminded me of Hank. And now it was ruined. That seemed darkly poetic.

Why hadn't I brought an extra dress?

After several minutes under the dryer, I surveyed the damage and decided the dress looked good enough to make it through the rest of the party.

So far, this night wasn't going as planned.

Hank was waiting at my table. He pointed at a fresh drink. "I ordered you another one. Is it okay if I share this table with you?"

"Of course, *dear*." I sipped my drink. "I'm surprised you aren't throwing the bags at the holes."

"Didn't feel like it. You okay?"

"I'm fine."

"You only say that when you're mad."

"Whatever would I have to be mad about?" I shook my glass. How had it gotten empty so quickly?

"You still upset about the room?"

"She said it was a suite." Clinging to that word helped make the weekend seem tolerable.

Hank glanced at the cabin. "Kind of."

Her description—mainly the word romantic—and his reaction hinted that a two-bedroom suite wasn't where we'd be spending the weekend.

"Hank, we haven't lived in the same house for over a year. I don't know how you conveniently forgot to mention the demise of our marriage in all that time." Smiling while I spoke, anyone watching would be fooled . . . except Haley.

"I don't know what you want me to do. I asked at the front desk again. They don't have any other rooms."

"If you'd said something *before*, this wouldn't be a problem."

"Did you want me to send out Christmas cards that read: Ho Ho Ho! My marriage lasted three months?" He shoved his hands in his pockets. "I messed up. Just like I do with everything else."

"Did you send out Christmas cards?"

He dragged his fingers through his hair. "It's like you don't even know me. Of course I didn't send out Christmas cards."

"So people think *I* didn't send out Christmas cards. You might've mentioned that before tonight."

"Nacha, I've lost track of all the ways I've ruined everything. Let me grab a pen and you can give me the list again." He leaned in close, and his cologne wrapped around me, reminding me of days and nights I'd tried to forget.

I blinked, snapping back to reality. "Do *not* play the martyr." I finished my drink. "But after this weekend, will you please say something? Aunt Joji wants to send us on a second honeymoon."

"Crap. Saying no to her isn't easy."

"You need to figure out how. I'm going to say goodnight to Haley and head to the room." How was I going to make it through the weekend?

Haley smiled and stepped away from the game as I approached. "You okay?"

I hugged her. "Everything tonight has been beautiful. If

you don't mind, I'm going to head to my room. This dress is a mess."

"Hank told me about the room. I'm so sorry."

"We'll be fine. I'll throw a pillow at him if he snores." Throwing pillows might happen whether he snored or not.

Zach walked up, grinning. Being Hank's best friend made him privy to the whole situation, but I never knew what he was thinking. He leaned in to hug me. "Give him a chance." Whispered so even Haley couldn't hear, his words twisted my insides into knots.

Nodding, I turned and walked away in deliberate steps. Tears blurred my vision, and my one focus was making it to the cabin without crying in front of people. I'd given Hank a chance—I'd married the man, and then he chose a job opportunity over me. Time was supposed to heal all wounds, but the wound in my heart was still as raw and painful as the day he'd walked out the door, promising that the long-distance marriage wouldn't be bad. What had changed in the last year was my ability to act like I was okay. I'd mastered it. Or so I thought.

I even had Haley fooled.

But if I didn't get out of here, no one would be fooled. I'd already embarrassed myself enough tonight.

I blinked. Wind gusted again, and I spun around, holding down the front of my dress.

"Nacha!" Hank waved his arms.

My defenses couldn't handle talking to him right now. Forcing a smile, I closed my eyes, spun back around, and marched forward. The heel of my pump landed in a hole and snapped off. I grabbed at air as I toppled forward, and my feet flew out from under me. After only a split second of worrying about being upside down in a dress and how much it would hurt to land on the pebbled patio, my head plunged under the water.

My nightmares became real.

Gulping water, I kicked and flailed, struggling to find the surface. Why was this happening to me?

After what felt like hours, cold air slapped my face, and I sucked in air before sinking back under the water. My skirt billowed out in a circle, putting everything underneath on public display. But I cared more about breathing . . . and not drowning.

Regrets flashed before my eyes. The last fifteen months had been full of them.

Feeling pulled under again, I moved my arms faster.

"Don't fight me. I've got you." Hank wrapped a strong arm around me. "It's a little cold for swimming, don't you think? Or is pool water good for removing stains?"

I grabbed at his shirt. "Don't let me go." Terrified of having my face back under the water, I gripped his neck and shoulder.

In my head, he was a tree, and floodwaters were rising. I grabbed at him, trying to climb up high.

"Um, Nacha, if you don't calm down a little, we'll both sink." He peeled my fingers off his neck. "Trust me."

"I tried that once before." Lashing out wasn't helpful, but in my emotional state—something most people never saw—I couldn't find nice words to say . . . even to the man who'd just saved me from drowning. But I stopped trying to climb him.

"That's better. I'll get you out of here, then when we get back to our room, if you want to climb all over me, I'm completely open to that."

I slapped at his chest but only ended up splashing both of us.

"I thought you didn't like water in your face."

By the time we made it to the stairs at the shallow end, the dinner-party guests surrounded the pool.

"Nacha, are you okay?" Haley sounded genuinely worried.

Hank pulled me against him as I started to shiver. "She's fine. Just a little drenched."

Aunt Joji waved everyone away. "She's in good hands. Let her be." She held out towels. "What do you need me to do?"

Hank helped me out of the pool and wrapped a towel around me. "Stay with her a second. I'm going to dive in and grab our phones."

I waved at Haley. "I didn't mean to cause a scene. I tripped." Determined to get away, I trudged across the patio. The pebbles hurt my feet, and my beautiful shoes—part of them, at least—lay at the bottom of the pool.

"Wait for Hank, dear." Aunt Joji wrapped her skinny fingers around my arm. Fighting her wasn't worth the effort.

Drying my face with the towel, I waited.

Hank waved off her offer of a towel as he climbed out of the pool. Dripping wet, he scooped me up. "Goodnight, Aunt Joji."

I pressed a hand to his chest, ready to demand that he put me down, but there was no fight in me. And his chest felt amazing. I leaned my head on his shoulder, no longer holding back my tears. "Why are you carrying me?"

"Because that dress was not made for being worn wet and half of your heel is still stuck in the patio."

I didn't want to think about the wet dress clinging to me in all the wrong places. "Thank you."

Hank's shoes squished and squeaked as he carried me. And if the entire scene weren't so horrible, I would've laughed at the trail of water we left behind.

Hank was the only person at the party who knew about my fear of water, and he hadn't hesitated to jump in and save me. "You scared me, Nacha. I tried to stop you, but you ignored me."

"I was hurrying away because I didn't want anyone to see

me upset." A breeze whipped at us, and I snuggled closer. "They'll assume I had too much to drink. It's so embarrassing. What's worse is that tonight is the first time I've had any alcohol since . . ." I glanced back toward the patio, hoping the festivities had returned to normal.

Aunt Joji waved. Hank and I would be on display all weekend. And my dip in the pool only made it worse.

"Please don't cry." He stopped on the porch and looked down at me, our faces only inches apart. "I'm sorry about everything. As soon as I change clothes, I'll go find Aunt Joji and tell her we aren't together anymore."

This weekend was about Haley and Zach, not me.

I shook my head. "Not tonight. It can wait until after the wedding. Let's not cause any more of a ruckus."

He shifted me in his arms. When he spoke, I could feel his breath tickling my lips. "I promise I'll be good." His eyes crinkled at the corners, an expression that always made my knees weak.

If I moved even a fraction of an inch, our lips would meet.

One thing hadn't changed in fifteen months. Hank was hot. Maybe hotter than the day he walked out.

Walked out.

That thought jolted me back to reality. "You can put me down."

"Once we're inside." He dragged the keycard across the corner of the towel on my hip, then held it next to the little black box. Thankfully, the light turned green, and he opened the door. "It isn't exactly a suite. I know Aunt Joji called it that, but . . ."

I shoved on his chest, trying not to think about his well-defined pecs, the ones his wet shirt did little to hide. When my feet hit the floor, I whipped around.

In the middle of the room a round jacuzzi tub was sunk into the floor. Above it, a crystal chandelier glowed, sending dapples of light dancing on the walls. A large king-sized bed sat at the far end of the room. Near the door, a love seat was positioned in front of a fireplace. And a bottle of champagne sat nestled in an ice bucket on the small table near the love seat.

"There's only one bed. And that isn't even a full couch."

He chuckled as he unbuttoned his shirt. "I figured you'd mention the jacuzzi tub first."

"What are you doing?"

He looked at me like I was speaking a different language. "Taking off my wet clothes."

"Here?" I sounded unreasonable even to myself.

"Would you rather I drip water all over the room? You don't have to watch." He shrugged off his dress shirt and let it puddle on the tile.

You don't have to watch. He was completely mistaken. I could pretend not to watch, but I did have to watch. Compelled was the word I'd use.

"I think my luggage is still in Haley's room." I exercised my peripheral vision. "And my purse. It must be in the pool or maybe beside it."

He yanked off his t-shirt.

I didn't mean to sigh.

His lips twitched at one corner, but other than that, he acted like he didn't notice. Continuing to undress, he unbuckled his belt. "I brought your stuff in earlier. It's on a luggage holder on the other side of the bed."

"You knew this was a quaint, romantic honeymoon cottage and didn't tell me? Are you the one who ordered the champagne?"

He sucked in a deep breath and let it out slowly. He did that when he was trying not to argue.

Instead of saying something to pacify me, he inched closer. "You can't stand champagne. Why would I order it?

And for the record, this seemed like a better place to have our little couples spat. Are you going to get out of your clothes or just stand there pretending not to watch me?"

The Hank riddled with self-pity wasn't attractive. But this one—the one who snapped back and called my bluff, the one who knew me—still made me heart go flippity-flop.

It would be a long weekend.

CHAPTER 2

"Now that you've changed, go out to the patio for a minute." I pointed at the back door, forcing my teeth not to chatter.

He shook his head. "I'm leaving. You can change without worrying about what I'll see." He yanked on a sweatshirt.

"Where are you going? You're *in* the wedding. You're the one giving her away. You can't leave. Haley would be crushed. And Zach would never forgive you." Desperate to change his mind, I hurried toward him.

"Careful! It's slick." Hank had a knack for timing his warnings all wrong.

Slipping, I grabbed for the nearest thing to keep me from falling. Clutching handfuls of Hank's sweatshirt, I steadied myself.

He wrapped an arm around my waist. "Miss me, do you?"

Lying through my teeth, I shook my head. "No. Let me go." Then I grabbed him again. "But you can't leave. Please don't."

"I'm a bit hurt that you think I'd miss their big day. I'm

leaving *temporarily* to go find rice. I'm hoping my phone is salvageable."

"Oh." I'd made a fool of myself. Again.

His gaze swept over my dress. "I'm not sure what you're worried about me seeing. That wet dress doesn't hide much." He winked. "While I'm gone, you can take that off and shower in *privacy*."

Earlier, every little thing Hank did was tainted with a hint of an apology. He'd acted that way since I'd served him with divorce papers—every message and every encounter. But after rescuing me, the confident man I'd married showed up again. Could he see the effect he had on me?

"Will you get enough for my phone too?"

"Sure." He jingled his keys, then disappeared out the door.

The room seemed colder without him in it.

I peeled off my dress and let it fall next to Hank's clothes. The wet mess would still be there after my hot shower.

With the bathroom door closed and hot water streaming from the shower head, the room filled with steam. I stepped under the hot water and pulled in a deep breath. Slowly releasing the breath while water cascaded over my hair and down my body, I found my center. My muscles thanked me for relaxing.

After standing in the warmth for a few minutes, I washed my hair, cleaned up, and stepped out of the shower. With a plush white towel wrapped around me, I stepped out of the bathroom. Humming, I crossed the room, leaned over my suitcase, and found something suitable for sleeping. I hadn't packed with company in mind.

"Ahem. Want me to leave again?" Hank's voice held a tease I hadn't heard in far too long. But it wasn't welcome right now.

Without turning around, I tugged at the bottom edge of the towel. "I didn't know you were back."

"Must've been a nice, long shower."

I gathered clothes into my arms. "It was relaxing." How long had I been in there?

"I miss you, Nacha." The gravel in his voice sent heat radiating over my skin. "I'm not sure what happened to the woman I married. You've walled yourself off. And I miss you so much it hurts."

My carefully constructed walls weren't keeping out my pain tonight. A conversation about what had happened was long overdue, but we couldn't talk here. Not the night before the wedding. "I can't talk about that right now. Not dressed in a towel in this romantic cabin. I just can't." I turned and met his gaze. "I'm sorry."

He gave me a weak smile, but there was a sadness filling his gaze. "I guess suggesting you take off the towel would only get me in trouble."

"Hank, I—"

"Go get dressed. Then we can sit here by the fire and talk about something else."

"I need to pick up—"

"Already cleaned up the wet mess. Our clothes are hanging on the back patio. Your purse is on the table. It landed beside the pool."

"Thank you." I slipped back into the bathroom. The pajamas I brought were very short and almost see through. What seemed suitable moments ago wasn't what I wanted to wear while sitting beside Hank in front of a romantic crackling fire.

"Need to borrow one of my t-shirts?" If the man was so good at reading my mind, why hadn't he admitted that he never should have left?

"Yes, please."

When he knocked, I opened the door wide enough to stick out my arm. He pushed soft cotton into my hand.

His shirt was so big, it fell to the hem of my floral, lace-trimmed pajama shorts. But it was much better than the thin, white camisole top that went with the set.

I pulled open the door.

"They had a bottle of the Spanish red wine you like." Dressed in pajama pants and a threadbare t-shirt, he held out a glass.

Walking around the jacuzzi and past the little sofa, I accepted the glass on my way to the hearth. "This fire feels good."

"Thought you might like it after your swim." He took a swig of his favorite beer. "Our phones are buried in rice in that plastic container over there."

"Thanks."

Quiet seconds ticked by.

He stared at the fire, and I sipped my wine.

If we were going to talk, I'd have to start a conversation. "How has it been with Zach dating Haley? I know her side. You weren't exactly excited about the relationship in the beginning."

He tilted his head back and chuckled. "After being such a jerk, I'm surprised Haley forgave me. But it's been good. I know things will change even more after tomorrow."

"I can't imagine you and Zach not being friends."

"Me either." He picked at the corner of the label. "I want them to be happy. I don't want them to end up . . ."

Like us. I waited, giving him all the time he needed to finish the sentence, but he never did.

Hank rubbed his face. "Zach is completely smitten. I've lost count of how many times he's shown up at the house with flowers."

"Girls like flowers, Hank."

"In the beginning, yes. But even after he'd proposed, he

kept bringing them. She'd already said yes." He shrugged. "But what do I know?"

"No one can accuse you of being a sappy romantic." I pulled in another sip of my wine and closed my eyes as the flavors came alive on my tongue. "Do you like working for the department in Schatz County?"

"Well enough." He finished off his beer. "I bought a deck of cards. Want to play?"

"War is about all the strategy I can handle tonight."

"Well, come sit over here. We can't play with you all the way over there."

I moved to the love seat. "Need me to shuffle?"

"Don't trust me?"

"I think we covered that earlier tonight."

He ended the shuffle with a bridge, then cut the deck with one hand. "I did get us out of the pool."

"Thank you for that."

He dealt the cards. "Ace is high."

"I know how to play war." I took another sip of wine, then set my glass on the little table.

"Clearly."

Trying not to start a fight, I ignored his comment. "What happened to the champagne?"

"I gave it to someone who'd want it."

"Who?"

He turned over his top card. "Does it matter?"

"Not really. I was just curious who you'd been talking to." I flipped over my top card, then slid both cards face up onto the bottom of my deck.

"Aunt Joji." He laid a card on the cushion.

"Why did you give it to her? I don't want her to be hurt that we didn't want it."

He shook his head. "I simply told her you didn't like champagne. Why would that hurt anyone's feelings?"

"I just don't want her to think I'm ungrateful."

"She doesn't. Are you going to make me sleep on the floor? There's no way I'll fit on this little sofa."

"Play the game."

"That would be easier to do if you'd put down a card." A teasing smile cut across his handsome face. "Am I distracting you?"

I slapped a card onto the cushion. "I win again."

Over and over, we threw down cards. He won as often as I did.

"Both sevens. This means war!" Hank laughed and put three cards face down before adding the last card face up. When he saw the ace, he smacked the cushion just as I put my cards down.

His victory celebration sent the cards flying. Some fell between the cushions.

He gathered up the cards. "This love seat isn't working."

"There isn't a table in here other than this little one."

"We'll move the game to the bed. Plenty of room up there."

I swung wide around the hot tub as I padded over to the bed. If this was his way of making it less weird when we crawled into bed to sleep, I had to give him credit for the good idea.

Game play resumed.

For an hour, we threw down cards.

His deck had gotten thicker. I was down to ten cards.

"Remember that night when we were camping and played Texas Hold 'em half the night?" Hank continued playing cards without looking up.

I remembered. That was the night I knew I was in love. A week later, he'd proposed. "I lost after going all in." The symbolism made me heart sick.

We both laid down threes, then put down our war cards.

This time fives sent us into another battle. In the end, I slapped down the high card.

"You won that round." He yawned. "Let's call it for tonight. We both have to be happy and sociable tomorrow."

"You don't want to play until someone loses their whole deck?"

"There doesn't always have to be a winner and a loser, Nacha." He held out his hand.

I slipped my fingers into his palm. "Maybe tomorrow night we can talk."

"I'd like that." He stared at our joined hands.

When his gaze cut to the cards in my other hand, a light went off in my head. "You put your hand out for my cards, didn't you?"

He nodded. "But I always like the feel of your hand in mine."

I plopped my deck into his palm. "Make sure you stay on your side of the bed."

CHAPTER 3

Warm and comfortable, I didn't want to open my eyes. As my morning fog cleared, I realized the reason for the warmth. Shoving Hank's arm off me, I sat up. "You didn't stay on your side."

He opened one eye. "Did too."

"But you—" I shut my mouth when I saw that my side of the bed was empty.

"Not gonna lie. I liked having company on my side."

I crawled to my side and climbed out of bed. "I have to eat something and start getting ready." By something I meant dark chocolate and hopefully coffee.

Yawning, he stretched bare arms into the air. When had he taken off his shirt? That chest . . . and those arms. He'd spent a lot of time working out. "I'll go get you something. Give me a second in the bathroom, then it's all yours for as long as you need it."

"Thank you. I'm sorry I accused you."

"Accused me of cuddling you? Guilty." He rolled out of bed, and thankfully was still wearing pajama pants. "But as I recall, there was no rule about that."

I stared at my suitcase, thinking through what I'd need. "My dress! I left it in Haley's room."

"If you don't have any issue with me seeing the dress before the wedding, I'll get it from her room while I'm out getting breakfast." He winked before closing himself in the bathroom.

"You aren't funny."

Laughter sounded from the other side of the door.

Somebody familiar and alluring had replaced the sniveling, apologetic Hank, and I missed this man more than I'd allowed myself to admit. But attraction—for that matter, even love—wasn't the same as trust.

I twisted my hair and pinned it up on my head with a clip. Today I'd be spending hours with Hank, and I needed to steel myself against this urge to give him another chance. My heart ached too much to let him in again.

The pieces of my heart were being held together with Scotch tape, and one good shake would make all those pieces crumble again. My heart might not be repairable a second time.

I slipped the chocolate bar out of my purse, thankful it hadn't been soaked by pool water. Letting the rich cocoa melt on my tongue, I closed my eyes.

The door creaked, but I didn't open my eyes. Retreating to a place of calm required focus.

"Watching you makes me want a taste."

So much for quiet.

He still didn't have a shirt on.

I held out the chocolate bar. "Break off a piece. I'll share."

"Not like that." He rubbed his thumb on my lip.

Throwing myself into his arms wouldn't change what happened. It would only complicate everything.

I brushed past him and put distance between us. "Thanks for getting breakfast and coffee."

Without turning around, he pulled on a shirt. "Anything to make you happy."

His back was just as fine as his chest, and if I didn't stop looking, I'd start touching. Then I wouldn't be ready for the wedding on time. And things would be complicated.

The hardest part of resisting him was the secret I carried, the secret I was too embarrassed and too afraid to admit. He wasn't my ex. Because I'd never turned in the divorce papers, the gorgeous man who'd shared my bed last night was my lawfully wedded husband.

Maybe tonight we'd have a chance to tackle a long-overdue conversation. I needed to set the man free and explain why I hadn't done it a year ago.

LOOKING OVER MY SHOULDER AT THE MIRROR, I CONTORTED, trying to reach the zipper. No matter which way I turned, I couldn't zip my dress.

I opened the bathroom door. "Will you help me? I can't get it zipped."

Hank stared, his smile widening every millisecond. "Wow. Yeah. Sure." His inability to string two words together flattered me.

"Just the zipper. No h—" I pinched my lips together and pulled my hair over my shoulder.

His breath tickled my ear as he leaned in close. "You were going to say *hanky-panky*, weren't you?"

"Please just zip it up." Thinking about the happy three months of our marriage and the silly things we used to say wasn't what I needed right now.

"Yes, ma'am." His fingers brushed my bare back.

I inhaled sharply, torn between remembering and wanting to forget.

"You don't have to suck in. It fits."

"Please just do it already."

I'd seen turtles cross the road faster than he moved that zipper up my back.

"You look incredible, Nacha. Absolutely stunning."

I spun around and adjusted his bow tie. "You don't look so bad yourself. That tux is…" It was hot, but I wasn't going to say that. "You've been working out?"

"Thanks for noticing." He rested a hand on my hip. "Will you dance with me?"

Picking at invisible dust on his jacket, I avoided his gaze. "Now?"

"I meant later, but now is good too." He reached into his pocket, then shook his head. "I'll have to sing something. Our phones are still in rice."

I patted his chest and finally braved eye contact. "I'll dance with you at the reception."

"Thank you. I asked here so you wouldn't feel like you *had to* say yes." He smiled and held out his arm. "You ready?"

Wrapping my fingers around his bicep, I nodded.

It was time to watch Haley and Zach say the words I'd never say again.

CHAPTER 4

*S*tanding at the front, I inhaled as the music changed. Hopefully, my waterproof mascara would do its job. The wedding march began playing, and the doors at the back opened.

Walking up the aisle on Hank's arm, Haley beamed.

Zach hadn't taken a breath since she'd appeared in the doorway. I'd never seen his smile that wide.

Hank stopped at the front and hugged Haley. That had me tearing up, but when Hank threw his arms around Zach, I nearly lost it.

Stepping into position between Zach and Adam, Hank took his place as the best man, then wiped his eyes. Tears were uncommon for him, and seeing them in his eyes did funny things to my heart.

I couldn't spend the entire wedding staring at Hank. I turned my focus to Haley and Zach.

The ceremony didn't drag out. That was one thing I loved about Haley. She wasn't about the fluff. The ceremony was only as long as it needed to be.

It seemed like only minutes before Zach was kissing his bride. Guests laughed when her feet left the floor.

Then Eve quickly handed over the bouquet and straightened the train. As the minister presented Mr. and Mrs. Gallagher to the world, Eve nudged me toward her spot. "Switch with me. I'll walk out with Adam."

I couldn't blame her for wanting to walk down the aisle with her husband. But walking down the aisle with my ex wasn't my first choice. "Sure."

Hank stepped to the middle and offered me his arm. When I clutched it, he laid his hand on mine. "My little sister is married."

I squeezed his arm, smiling up at him. "The ceremony was beautiful." The shutter clicks reminded me that almost everything that happened today would be captured in photos.

He led me to the room where the wedding party gathered to wait for picture time. It would be a few minutes until the guests made their way to the reception room. Then the photographer could take photos.

He glanced around the room until his gaze landed on a tissue box. With a tissue in his fist, he wiped his eyes again. "I feel like a ninny. This isn't what I expected."

I rubbed his back. "It's sweet."

"Sweet? Fabulous. I think that's equivalent to nice, isn't it?" He quirked an eyebrow.

With my lips near his ear, I whispered so only he'd hear me. "Sweet looks good on you, Hank." Why was I flirting with him?

My breath caught when I met his gaze. I'm not sure what I expected to see, but I wasn't prepared for the heat and hope swirling in his brown eyes.

"I should check my makeup before we do pictures."

"You look great." He touched my arm. "Really."

"I need to—I'll be back." I made my way to the ladies' room and stared in the mirror.

For most of a year, I'd stayed away from him because around him, I turned to mush. Just a look lit me up. And when he touched me, I wanted to wrap my body around his.

But that would only lead to more hurt. I couldn't even figure out how to deal with the hurt I was already dragging around.

When I walked back out after reminding myself that there'd be no second chances, I couldn't have said what color my lipstick was. My mind was so wrapped up with thoughts of Hank, I hadn't really seen anything in the mirror.

At the reception, as the dance floor filled with couples, Hank stood and held out his hand. "Would you like to dance?"

"Yes. That would be nice." I didn't want to change my mind now after saying yes this morning.

We held hands as we walked toward the dance floor.

He slipped an arm around me, and I slid my hand into his. He'd taken me dancing on our first date. It was one of his many talents. Following his lead, it was easy to lose myself in the music, letting his arms and the rhythm of the song carry me around the dance floor.

With every song, the distance between us shrank.

Hank nodded toward a guy on the other end of the dance floor. "What's his name? I should know this."

"Everyone calls him Harper. I think that's his last name. He's a good friend of Adam's."

Hank crinkled his nose, then laughed. "He's the guy who went out with Haley."

"Yes, which makes me wonder why he was even invited to the wedding."

"That's easy. Zach has a plan. Harper was invited to the party where Zach popped the question. This is just part two."

"Zach is gloating? That's just silly."

Hank shrugged. "Harper seems like a nice guy. At least the few times we've met."

For a few minutes, we didn't talk. It became harder to keep my distance. The longer our bodies moved in coordinated motion, the more I wanted to rest my head on his shoulder and feel his arm tighten around me.

"Is business going well?"

"It is. We're almost completely booked for the next few months. And I had an author contact me about doing a shoot for cover photos."

"Romance novels with shirtless guys? I can model for you if that would help."

"Keep your shirt on. She writes about mermaids and cat shifters."

"Can't help you with that." He twirled me and pulled me close again.

"Haley said the job in Montana didn't work out."

His body tensed. "Right."

Why had I brought that up? He'd wanted that job so desperately. Why had he only stayed three months?

"I bet the house will be quiet without Haley around."

He shrugged. "She was always at Zach's anyway, but yeah. I'm making a few changes that I haven't mentioned to her yet."

"Don't you think you should tell her? She's part owner of the house, right?"

"Mom and Dad left it to both of us, but I'm adding value. She won't care." His grin begged me to ask what upgrades he'd planned.

"What are you going to do?"

"Putting in a pool and hot tub." He winked. "But I won't make you swim."

"Make me?"

He kissed my forehead. "I can't make you do anything you don't want to do."

The music slowed, and I gave into temptation and leaned my head on his chest.

"Have you dated?" Why was he asking me that? And now?

I shook my head.

He let go of my hand and lifted my chin with one finger. "I know we need to talk. But know this, I won't even *think* of dating until *you* tell me it's over. Not some papers that need to be signed. I want to hear the words out of *your* mouth."

We'd hardly spent time in the same room in over a year. And our goodbye was when he left for that stupid job. After having him served with divorce papers, I'd ignored all his calls. But here he was telling me there wasn't anyone else . . . and wouldn't be until I called an end to things.

This man made me feel alive.

I wasn't ready to tell him it was over.

In fact, my mouth had other ideas. Ignoring all determination that there would be no second chances, my body cheered as I inched up and pressed my lips to his.

His arms wrapped around me, and couples danced past us as we kissed.

Memories of our past fueled my hunger for him. He deepened the kiss and moved us off the dance floor.

I pulled away, scared I was making a mistake. Would my tape hold? Could a heart heal?

"As much as I want to continue that—in our room—leaving now would be in bad taste. Looks like she's getting ready to toss the bouquet." Hank trailed his fingers down my bare back as we walked toward our table.

Too antsy to sit, I stood, watching.

His arms circled my waist. "Aren't you glad you don't have to be out there?"

"More than you know." Even before I knew Hank, I hated this part of the wedding.

I was never one that believed in tingling when people touched, but when he dropped kisses on my neck, every inch of my body felt electrified.

He brushed his clean-shaven cheek against mine. "I wasn't sure what to expect from today—besides them getting married, obviously—but this is more than I could've ever hoped. And I'm not assuming this changes *everything*, but I've spent a year hoping you'd give me another chance."

"We'll need to take it slow. I know I didn't really make that clear minutes ago."

He chuckled. "I didn't mind at all. And I can do slow." His lips brushed my ear. "Like molasses."

Heat spread over my skin. If he kept talking like that, I'd turn as red as my dress.

He stood with his arms around me while other people caught the bouquet and garter.

I titled my head up. "What time are they headed out?"

"Later. They just didn't want the guests to feel like they had to stay for hours."

"Is Haley going to play Cornhole in her wedding dress?"

"Maybe. That'd be funny." He scanned the room as several guests said their goodbyes to Zach and Haley.

I patted Hank's chest. "I'm going to visit the ladies' room. Be right back."

He handed me the keycard. "In case you need it. Some of the doors around here need room keys to open them." He kissed me before I stepped away, and every movement of his lips said to hurry back.

I slipped out a side door. Just before I reached the powder

room, Aunt Joji's voice caught my attention. I stopped near the corner and listened as she talked to the guy at the front desk.

"Thank you all for everything. I'm going to settle the bill now. But I have that one cabin for tomorrow night also."

"For tonight, do you need all the other rooms?"

"No, I just needed y'all to be full last night. One night did the trick." Her laugh echoed in the lobby.

I turned around and walked out the door on the far end of the building. Following the pebbled path, I made my way to my cabin. If I hurried, I could be packed and gone before Hank even realized I was missing.

He'd tricked me.

Who else besides Aunt Joji was in on it?

All the passion from moments ago morphed into fury. I pressed the key card to the little box, glad Hank had given me the key.

I shoved clothes and makeup into my suitcase. But when I picked up the engraved silver bowl Haley had given me, I stopped. Leaving now would be selfish. How would that look?

Rude.

That's how it would look.

Hoping Zach and Haley would decide they needed to leave soon, I set my luggage near the door and walked back to the reception.

The next few hours would be awkward.

CHAPTER 5

As soon as Haley and Zach drove away, I made my way across the reception room toward Aunt Joji. A very quiet Hank followed me.

"Aunt Joji, thank you so much for everything. The wedding was beautiful." I gave her a polite hug, resisting the temptation to shake her.

Aunt Joji patted my cheek. "You're so welcome. I do hope the two of you enjoy the cabin tonight *and* tomorrow night."

I smiled instead of answering.

As I walked to the cabin, Hank remained my silent shadow.

He held the key card to the little black box, then pushed open the door. When his gaze landed on my suitcase, his brow furrowed. "What's going on? One minute you're kissing me, then after a trip to the ladies' room, you will hardly look at me. When did you come back in here to pack?"

I inhaled, refusing to cry. "Why don't you go find Aunt Joji and drink to your great success? The trick worked. Shove them into the same room, and Nacha will change her mind and forgive everything."

He threw his hands in the air. "What are you talking about?"

"Aunt Joji rented all the vacant rooms so that there wouldn't be any left. That's why we had to stay in here together. How could you?" Tears stung my eyes. I wouldn't be able to keep my emotions in check for long.

He stepped in front of the door and leaned his face close to mine. "I didn't know, Nacha. I would *never* do that to you."

"Really? You didn't plan for us to share a big comfy bed and end up on the same side?"

"What happened on that dance floor was real and genuine. For me and for you. I know you, Nacha." He clenched his jaw. "Please don't do this to me again."

"Do this to *you*? How heartless of me." I picked up my suitcase. "Move."

"What should I tell Aunt Joji about the second honeymoon?"

"I don't care. Tell her whatever you want. Get the tickets and take someone else."

Fire burned in his eyes. "You don't mean that."

"I do, Hank. *It's over.*" Saying the words out loud felt like someone had taken a sledgehammer to my heart.

He shifted out of the way without looking up.

If there were tears, I didn't want to see them.

By the time I'd wrestled my suitcase into the car, unstoppable tears streamed down my cheeks. I climbed into the driver's seat and started the engine. The drive home was only forty-five minutes. I just needed to hold it together a little while longer.

I backed out of the parking space and made the mistake of glancing toward the cabin. Hank stood on the porch, his bow tie hanging loose and his hands shoved in his pockets.

If he hadn't planned the grand deceit, who did? It hurt to think Haley had been in on it. But how else did Aunt Joji know?

Kicking up gravel, I tore out of that parking lot. The faster I could put distance between me and that man, the faster my life could move onto the next chapter.

Inconveniently, my mind jumped to what I'd said. *Take someone else.* Thinking about him going on vacation with another woman made me want to hurl. There was nothing ladylike about that image, and I laughed. If anyone had seen me cackling while I sobbed, they'd swear I'd lost it.

Once I hit the highway, I pressed down hard on the gas pedal.

Had I really told him it was over? Did I believe that? Moments ago, I did. But now? I pounded on the steering wheel and turned up the radio. Sobbing, I swiped at my eyes as I barreled down the road.

Twenty minutes down the road, red and blue lights flashed behind me. I pulled off to the shoulder and wiped my eyes. In the side mirror, I watched the deputy walk toward my window.

I breathed in deep as I rolled down the window.

"Evening. I'm Deputy Gallagher." He blinked several times. "Hi, Nacha, right?"

"Yes, hi, Eli."

He rubbed the back of his neck. "Do you know why I pulled you over?"

Because the universe hates me? I swallowed, hoping my voice wouldn't sound broken and scratchy. "I'm not sure. Was I speeding?"

"Yes, you were exceeding the speed limit. Could I see your license and insurance, please?"

"Yes." Why wouldn't the tears quit falling? I reached into my purse and dug around until I found what I needed.

It didn't help that he eyed me the entire time.

"Does Hank know where you are?"

Smiling, I shook my head. "Probably not."

"Are you okay?" He clearly wasn't fooled by the smile on the woman with mascara streaked down her face.

"I'm fine. I just didn't realize I was driving too fast."

His brow pinched. "Should I call—"

Why did I have to get pulled over in the county where Zach and Hank both worked? And by Zach's cousin?

Maybe I could distract him from talking about calling Hank. "I was just on my way home from Haley's wedding."

"Did it go okay? Did something bad happen?"

"The wedding was beautiful. They left just a bit ago for the honeymoon." Was it really so strange for someone to be sobbing after a wedding?

He grinned. "I couldn't make it since I was working. I hope they're really happy."

"Me too."

"Are you sure you don't want to—"

"I'm Hank's ex." The words tasted bitter. Why had I said that?

He hadn't mentioned Hank, but like a fool, I brought it up.

I wiped at another tear.

Eli ran his fingers through his hair, clearly unsure about what to do. "Are you sure you're okay to drive? Maybe you should call *someone*."

"I'll slow down."

He handed back my ID and insurance paper. "I'm letting you off with a warning this evening. Please be careful and do slow down."

"I will. Thank you, Eli." My choked-out words probably didn't help convince him I was okay, but it was the best I could do.

I made sure not to slam down the accelerator when I pulled away. The last thing I needed to do was spray the poor deputy with gravel. As it was, he'd probably tell all the guys about Hank's crazy ex in the bridesmaid dress, who looked like she was ready for a Halloween party.

I'd just avoid booking photography shoots in this county. Haley could cover anything that needed to be done around here. If I didn't come into this county, I'd never see these guys again. Probably. Unless Haley invited Zach's cousin to a party or something. But I'd just have to cross that bridge when I came to it.

Keeping my speed just under the limit, I drove home. As I passed the San Antonio city limit sign, a horrible thought registered. My phone was still buried in rice back at the cabin.

I had to figure out how to get my phone back.

When I made it to the house, I hauled my suitcase inside. But before unpacking, I slipped off my dress, then padded into the kitchen to get the coconut oil. Why was it so difficult to get off a stick-on bra?

Finally, after a bit of trouble getting it unstuck, I pulled on a sweatshirt and a pair of cotton shorts. I emptied my suitcase, dropping dirty clothes in the hamper and putting clean clothes where they belonged. When I picked up Hank's shirt, the sobs started again. I tossed it in the hamper.

Where was my bra? I'd taken it off because it didn't work with the dress, and I'd—Crap. My favorite bra was hanging on the doorknob in the bathroom at the cabin.

Would Hank even notice? And if he did, would he give it back? It wasn't like he needed it.

And my yellow dress was still out on the patio where he'd hung it to dry. It was embarrassing how much of my clothing had been left behind.

I unwrapped a chocolate bar. I might need all twelve to get me through the evening.

After everything I'd said would it be weird to call him? I didn't see that going well.

But if I wanted my phone, my dress, and bra, I had no choice.

At half past seven, it was too early to crawl in bed. I didn't want to be home by myself because I'd only sit and stew. Now more than ever, everything reminded me of Hank. We'd signed on this house a week before the wedding.

When I sent over divorce papers, he'd scribbled a note at the bottom apologizing and telling me I could have the house and anything else I wanted.

I grabbed my keys, pulled on shoes, and ran to the car. It wasn't exactly shorts weather, but changing would take too much time.

Ten minutes later, I walked into my mama's kitchen. I knew I'd find her here in this room, which is exactly why I came. Mama's kitchen offered a comfort only rivaled by . . .

The memory of Hank's arm wrapped around me popped in my head, and I worked to dismiss the thought. Right now, that was the opposite of comforting.

"Hi. I wasn't sure if you'd be home."

"Of course I'm home. It's Saturday night. Where else would I be?" She wiped her hands on her apron.

"Mind if I stay for a little while?"

"*Mijita*, you don't have to ask. Have a snack." She shuffled across the kitchen in her favorite blue slippers.

"Thanks, Mama. What are you making?"

"*Buñuelos.*"

"My favorite."

She turned around as I sat down. "Nacha, what's wrong?"

"I'm okay." The tears had finally stopped, and I felt better than I had in hours.

Mama grabbed a rag and wet it in the sink. "Your face has makeup streaked all over it. What made you cry?" She wiped at my face like I was five.

"I saw Hank at the wedding."

She backed up and shook her head. "I don't understand you, Nacha. It isn't like the man *cheated* on you or *hit* you. You're being stubborn." She shuffled back to the stove, then returned with a plate of *buñuelos* in one hand and a shaker of cinnamon sugar in the other. "Eat. I'll make more."

Her dismissal hurt. She was right that Hank wouldn't cheat, and the man would die before ever raising a hand to me. But he'd hurt me. And I didn't know how to deal with the pain.

"I thought you of all people would understand. He left me. Just like Papá left us."

Mama spun around, and a fire burned in her eyes. "Don't call him that. His name was Eric."

"Okay." I was shocked at her sharp response. "I just—he signed my birthday cards that way, so I—" I hadn't even taken a bite, and I was losing my appetite.

"*I* signed your cards that way. *I* sent them." She waved a hand, then turned back to the stove.

More of me crumbled.

"He didn't even send me cards?" I felt abandoned all over again. "Why did he leave?"

"Because your uncles threatened to do him bodily harm if he showed up at the house again. Ever."

"Mama! That's crazy. Why haven't you ever told me this?"

"Is that why you are mad at Hank? Because a man you hardly knew left when you were too young to remember? Hank is nothing like him."

"Didn't it hurt you that he left?"

She waved her tongs. "What hurt was when he hit me. Know why he hit me? Because I told him I wouldn't tolerate cheating." She rubbed her cheek. "Once my brothers saw my bruise, they had words with him. Eric packed a bag and left the next day. It never happened again."

"How did you learn to trust after he left?" I desperately needed the answer to that question.

"Don't blame Hank for your father's sins." Mama dropped into a chair. "There were a few hard years. You were so little, and I prayed you wouldn't remember. Then I met Jeffrey, and there was a point when I had to trust him or lose him. And I didn't want to lose him."

Cinnamon fell to the table as I bit into my *buñuelo*. "He was a good husband."

"Very good. I miss him so much." She walked back to the stove, then turned to face me. "Don't let your pride get in the way."

"You're supposed to be on my side."

"Nonsense. I can choose whatever side I want." She sprinkled cinnamon sugar on the flaky treats she'd just pulled out of the oil. "Besides, I like Hank. He mows my grass each week."

"He what?"

"You should see a doctor and get your ears checked." She snickered.

"He comes here every week?"

"And I make him his favorite foods." She waggled a finger in my face. "Don't mess up my good deal."

I ate my way through three *buñuelos* before Mama swatted my hand. "Take some home. You'll be sick if you eat too many."

"When is he coming again?"

"It depends on his work schedule. Probably Friday."

I wasn't sure what to do with that information.

Mama hugged me. "I hope he doesn't find anyone else.

She might not like him helping his ex-mother-in-law. That would be unfortunate."

Now wasn't the time to admit what I'd said to Hank. But now, just maybe, I had a plan for getting my phone back and maybe my bra. Hank probably didn't even remember the clothes on the patio.

CHAPTER 6

Sunday, I emailed the model for my photo shoot, hoping Cami would check her email before assuming I'd flaked on her. We'd planned to meet up in the afternoon, but I always texted or called on the day of. That wasn't happening today.

As I looked over my pile of camera gear, someone knocked. I pulled the door open. "You got my message?"

Cami held up my bra. "Why is this hanging off your doorknob? And it has a note attached."

I snatched the bra out of her hand. "Is there a phone out here?"

"I don't see one. I thought the email said you'd lost your phone." She crossed her arms. "There's got to be a good story behind this. I want to hear it."

Who else was I going to tell? Mama was on Hank's side, and Haley had helped make a fool of me. "Come on in."

Cami followed me inside and surveyed the house from the entryway. "This place is really nice."

"Thanks."

"What does the note say?" She cocked her head and

pressed her hands together. "Please. You know my love life is a royal mess. My boss dumped me, and now I get to watch him flirt with his new assistant. I swear she's not even legally allowed to drink."

Being around Cami always made me laugh. "Hearing about my love life just might make you feel better. My ex left this outside for all the world to see. But he didn't bother leaving my phone, which I need." I unfolded the note and read it out loud.

Your mom has your phone. There was no way I was giving her your bra. And just like you did with the house, keep my t-shirt.

Cami's jaw dropped. "Wow. You do have it worse. Did you . . . did he . . . you know—how did he get your bra?"

I told her the whole sordid story.

She pressed a hand to her chest. "It's like the beginning of a Hallmark movie, but wait—he didn't cheat on you, did he?"

Why did that keep coming up?

"No, he didn't. He's not a cheater. But it's not like one of those sweet romance movies. It's like one of those late-night heartbreak movies. I told him it was over. That's why he hung my bra on my door for the whole neighborhood to see."

"Who cares what your neighbors think?"

"I live here. Don't you care what your coworkers think now that you and the boss aren't dating anymore?"

She shrugged. "I spend too much time convincing myself not to strangle him to care what other people think. If I can make enough from modeling gigs, I'll quit that job."

"Today's shoot is easy-peasy. No funny costumes. Just a woman standing in a field of flowers." I set the note on the mantle. "You ready?"

"What's he like?"

"Who?" I loaded the gear into my backseat.

She buckled into the passenger seat. "Your ex. I need to

find a new type. Dating the corporate types hasn't worked out for me."

"So now you're thinking about dating my ex?" I amped up the sarcasm, my stomach twisting at the thought.

"What? No! That's not what I meant. I just—what does he do?"

"He's a paramedic."

"Maybe I *should* think about it. I've never met one that wasn't totally swoon-worthy. And you said he wasn't a cheater. I've dated too many of those."

I stared at her, then slammed on the brakes when I realized the light was turning red. "Please tell me you're joking."

"Yes, I'm joking. But gosh, if you don't want him, why do you care?" Cami grinned. "Ignore that question. I'd rather not be murdered today."

"I don't care."

She giggled. "My mom showed me this old movie called The Princess Bride. Have you ever seen it?"

"I've seen it."

"Anyway, when you said you didn't care, I thought of that scene with the old woman." Cami messed up her hair and pointed at me. "Liar!"

"You can stop. I've seen the movie." Despite my irritation, I laughed. "You're crazy. You know that?"

"And apparently that isn't enough to snag a guy. What's the world coming to?"

"I don't know what to tell you about that." I checked my rearview mirror as I pulled into my favorite photography spot in Schatz County. When I promised myself I wouldn't come back here, I'd forgotten about this photo shoot.

"Did Haley ever convince that deputy who kept showing up that y'all had permission to be out here?"

"She married him."

"That's a bit extreme. Is he hot?"

I smacked her arm. "Is that all you ever think about?"

"No, but it's important to me. I don't want to be alone forever." She climbed out of the car and crossed her arms. "I should've grabbed a jacket."

I imagined the words stamped on my head. *Alone forever.* "We won't be out here long."

"You think a different deputy will come out today?" She glanced back toward the gate. "I'm thinking maybe I need a hero type."

"Move to your left." I clicked the shutter, catching the cute, dreamy look on her face. "Looks like you'll get your wish." After a few more shots, I turned around and smiled.

A marked deputy's vehicle stopped next to my car. The door opened, and Eli slid out. "We meet again."

Cami ran up behind me. "Who is that? Is he available? Because he is so hot."

"You know the guy Haley married? This is his cousin." I stepped forward to greet Eli. "Hello again. We have permission to be out here."

"I know. The dispatcher told all of us not to worry if we saw you or Haley out here." His gaze cut to Cami. "I recognized your car and wanted to ... um ... say hi."

He was smart, not exactly smooth, but very smart. "I'm glad you did. Have you met my friend Cami?"

"No, I haven't." He stuck out his hand, and that knee-buckling Gallagher grin spread across his face. "Eli Gallagher."

Her head bobbed up and down, and she smiled. "Hi."

"I can see y'all are busy with pictures. I don't want to interrupt."

I gave him a quick hug. After all, he was practically—almost like—family. "Thanks for stopping."

He tipped his hat, and Cami sighed.

It wasn't even spring, and love was in the air. Ugh.

TWO WORDS I'D NEVER SAY AGAIN

"Mama, it's me." I knocked on the front door as I pushed it open.

Laughing echoed from the kitchen. "I'm in the kitchen, but don't come in here. Stay where you are."

What was going on?

She walked into the living room and handed me my phone. "Need anything else? I have company."

"He's here, isn't he? I didn't see his truck."

She waved her hands. "Shh. You'll scare him off. He's helping me with my garden."

"You don't have a garden!" I moved to step around her.

"*Mijita*, don't cross me." She rarely used a sharp tone with me.

I backed up. "You're making me leave so that you can talk to him?"

"Yes, I'm glad you understand. We're planning my garden." She peeked into the kitchen and waved.

"Fine. I'll leave." I trudged out to my car. I didn't want to tell anyone about tonight. It was too embarrassing. My own mother chose my ex over me because he mowed her grass and promised her a garden.

Haley had Zach. Hank had my mother. That sounded all wrong. And Cami was well on her way to having Eli hooked. Who didn't have anyone? Me.

Growing up, I heard every Nacho joke middle school kids could dream up. They didn't even sound right substituting Nacha, but the kids did it anyway. And now so many seemed to fit. I'm Nacha friend. Nacha girlfriend. Nacha wife.

I spotted his truck parked a few houses down. He'd set me up. Again.

CHAPTER 7

After two weeks of avoiding my mother and trying to run the photography business alone, I was irritated and ready to unleash my frustration on Haley. That would have to wait until tomorrow when she'd finally be back in the office.

I washed out my bowl and tucked my dishes in the dishwasher. Cooking wasn't one of my talents, so I stuck with salad kits and instant oatmeal.

The doorbell rang, and I hurried to the door. Who would be showing up on a Sunday evening?

Aunt Joji stood on the porch wearing cuffed jeans and a *Raid Area 51* t-shirt. "I come bearing gifts."

"Hi!" My tongue felt knotted. "I, uh, didn't expect to see you."

Aunt Joji shifted an elaborately wrapped package on her hip. "May I come in?"

"Sure." I stepped back to let her enter. "Can I get you coffee or something else to drink?"

"Yes. Coffee would be great. As long as you don't poison

me with it." Her infectious laugh filled the room. "But maybe I deserve that."

"I'd never—"

"I know, dear." She rested a hand on my shoulder. "And please take this with all the love that's intended. I think you have a long list of nevers."

The truth of the words stung, but the audacity of her words set my brain on fire.

"If you just came to mock me, you can leave. I've had plenty of that." I crossed my arms, breathing in deep, wishing that my insides would stop quivering. I was mortified at my rudeness and proud that I'd spoken up for myself. Why did setting boundaries and being polite feel in opposition to each other?

Aunt Joji continued toward the kitchen, and I followed.

Since she wasn't leaving, I rinsed the carafe and filled the coffee maker with water.

She set the present on the table and sat down. "I'm not mocking you, Nacha. I used to be you."

The glass carafe slipped out of my hand, but I caught it before it smashed into the counter. "You what?"

The only sound in the room was the rumbling and burbling of the coffee maker.

"I'll tell you about that another day. This evening, I stopped by to bring you this"—she tapped the pretty package—"and to apologize."

I filled two mugs, then shuffled the cups, sugar, and half and half to the table. "You don't have to—" I stopped myself from dismissing her apology. "Who else knew about the plan?"

Aunt Joji added milk and sugar to her coffee. "The plan was all mine. Haley told me about the divorce. She said it made her sad because it was clear you and Hank still loved each other. She had no idea about any of the rest."

I blinked away the sting of tears. "I didn't know she thought that."

"Lots of people think that." She sipped her coffee, then added another cube of sugar. "Neither Haley nor Hank had any idea that I booked all the other rooms or that I intentionally put the two of you in the same romantic honeymoon cabin. Haley and Zach weren't going to use it. It seemed a waste to let it stay empty."

Aunt Joji's transparency made it easy to be honest with her. "I'll always love Hank. But sometimes love isn't enough. I need to be able to trust him, and I don't."

She nodded and drank more of her coffee. "Anywhere in the world—where would you go?"

"You don't have to give me anything because you weren't here for the wedding. I don't think you are playing favorites." I sipped my coffee. "I accept your apology."

"Where?" She tousled her red curls. "Easy question."

I didn't have to dream up an answer. There was one place I'd wanted to visit for years. Why put off telling her? "Madrid."

Smiling, she slipped an envelope out of her purse. "Two tickets to Madrid. The arrangements and accommodations are all listed in here. The dates can be changed to suit your schedule."

"I don't—how did you know?" As soon as the question left my mouth, I knew the answer. "Hank told you."

"After he shouted a few choice words at me—which I won't repeat—I asked him where'd you want to go. He said Madrid was where you'd talked about going because you wanted to photograph the city and because your grandmother had traced the family line back to that part of Spain. After telling me, he walked out of the room and slammed the door. I haven't talked to him since. Not for lack of trying."

"I'm sorry."

"Why are you apologizing? I'm the one who caused this mess. I should have just been honest, then locked you in a room together." Chuckling, she finished off her coffee. "I see what Haley talked about." Aunt Joji brushed away tears, then clasped my hand. "Love doesn't come around every day. Especially the kind you share with Hank. When it's gone and you can never get it back, the regret is suffocating. I don't want that to happen to you."

I resisted the urge to pull my hand away. It wasn't as if I could flip a switch. There was no magic that could make my heart not hurt. "I wish it were so simple."

"When you can't have what you wanted most, you learn everything is simple." She popped up. "Thank you for the coffee."

"I think maybe it's already too late. Suffocating describes how I've felt these last few weeks."

"Both of you are still alive. It's not too late." She dropped little teasers that made me want to know more of her story.

"I'd really like to hear about how you used to be like me."

She laid a card on the table. "This is my number. Call me, and we'll schedule dinner. My treat."

I flipped through the calendar in my head. "I'm free Thursday."

"I'll be out of town until just after Thanksgiving, but we'll find a date." She opened her arms. "Will you forgive me?"

I hugged her. "Of course." I picked up the tickets, ready to hand them back. "Would you give these to Hank?"

"Nope." She patted my cheek. "I won't interfere again, but I also won't make it easy for you to make a huge mistake."

"I'll call you."

She waved and walked out the front door.

Mind whirling, I peeled the tape off the present and unwrapped the shoe box. Inside was a new pair of heels that exactly matched the ones ruined by my tumble and dip in the pool. Tucked underneath them was a gift card to a shoe store.

I stared at the beautiful shoes that looked exactly like the ones that caused me pain when I wore them. It didn't stop me from putting them on whenever I had some event that required me to dress up.

My chest tightened as I thought about what she'd said. She wasn't there when I'd told Hank it was over. She didn't see the light in his eyes stamped out by the finality of my words.

I tossed the rest of my coffee down the sink.

Somehow, I had to figure out how to battle regret's suffocating grip.

It was too late.

Aunt Joji's comment about being like me didn't make sense. Nothing about me was like her. She fluttered through life not caring what people thought. Other people's opinions guided my every step.

When Hank left to take that job, I was sure people would think he cared more about his job than he did for me. Those presumed opinions, combined with issues about being left by my father, drowned out Hank's assurances that our relationship could handle being apart for a short time.

What was wrong with me?

I set the shoes in my closet, changed into Hank's t-shirt, and curled up in bed with my tablet to read something that would make me laugh.

Two chapters in, I gave up.

Anger and embarrassment had blinded me. If Aunt Joji hadn't shown up tonight, I'd have permanently damaged my friendship and business relationship with Haley. I'd scripted my complaints about her ruining my life and had been prepared to lob them at her in the morning.

The truth was, I'd ruined my marriage. And it was too late

to do anything about it. *It's over* weren't words that could be taken back.

Monday morning, I made it into the office early. I'd picked up breakfast tacos, doughnuts, and coffee on the way.

Haley was back from her honeymoon, and her short text said she planned to be at work today.

Not long after I arrived, Cami strolled in.

"Morning. I'm hoping your author friend needs lots of pictures because I quit my job."

"You what?" I pointed at the food, thankful I'd grabbed extras. "Help yourself."

Haley floated into the room, beaming. "Good morning!"

I hugged her. "Your smile is so bright, I might need to dim the lights."

She rolled her eyes, then zeroed in on the food. "Thank you for grabbing food. I was nearly late this morning and didn't have a chance to eat."

Asking why wasn't necessary. "Coffee's on your desk. Cami was about to tell me why she quit this morning."

Haley threw her arms around Cami. "Yay! I'm glad you aren't working with that creep anymore."

"Me too. He asked me out again. But he's still seeing the new assistant. I'd rather sell French fries than work with him." She bit into a doughnut. "I met your husband's cousin. Is he single?"

"Eli? Totally single." Haley unwrapped a breakfast taco.

The phone rang, and I jumped up.

Haley shook her head. "I'll get it." She ran into her office.

Cami dropped into a chair. "The bad thing about quitting—I'll probably have to move back home with my parents. Ugh. I hate the thought. I don't really want to leave

San Antonio, so if you know of anyone who is looking for a roommate, let me know. That would be a way better option."

"If I hear of anything." I had plenty of room, and a little bit of rent money would add breathing room to my budget. Keeping the house meant paying the mortgage, and all alone, that was stretching me.

"We have another booking. I'm hoping the calendar is up to date." Haley picked up a doughnut.

"It is." I inhaled half my cup of coffee. "While you were gone, I hardly got anything done. I spent most of my time between shoots answering the phone and returning calls. To get the calendar updated, I stayed until midnight on Friday."

"Midnight? On a Friday?" Cami shook her head. "That's crazy. You should be out having fun." She whipped around and faced Haley. "Know any hot guys Nacha might like?"

"Cami!" I threw a napkin at her. "I don't need a hot guy."

Haley's smile fell away. "I should get to work."

I didn't need to ask how Hank was doing. Thanks to Cami and Haley's reaction, I knew Hank wasn't doing well.

Cami slapped a hand over her mouth and gaped at me. "Oops! You were . . . married to her . . . brother. Sorry about that. I think I made it weird."

"You totally did." Haley gave a brusque nod. "Talk to you later." Her door closed, and the air chilled.

Cami followed me into my office. "I'm sorry about that. Sometimes I don't think about what I'm saying."

"I know." I shuffled through papers, trying to mentally prep for the week.

"But it sounds like he isn't doing great. Like maybe he misses you."

"Or he's mad at me. I've made several people upset."

She came around the desk and hugged me from behind. "We all love you, Nacha. You just don't make it easy. Thanks for breakfast. I'm going to crash at the coffee shop down the street and look for job openings."

"Bye. Good luck." I couldn't imagine what she meant about it not being easy to love me. Guarded wasn't the same as unlovable.

I spent the next two hours on and off the phone. Haley stayed in her office the whole time.

Just before noon, she knocked at my open door. "Want to grab lunch?"

"Sure. Is this business partners getting out of the office or friends needing to talk?" I picked up my purse.

"A little of both. I'm buying." She locked the door as we stepped outside. "But I'm not breaking up with you."

"That's a relief. Neither my emotions nor my pocketbook could handle that right now." I walked toward my car. Most of the time, I drove when we went anywhere.

Haley shook her head. "I'm driving today."

"Okay." I slid into her passenger seat. "What's up?"

"I don't want to be trying to edit photos at home every night. But the phones have gotten so busy, working at work is difficult."

"I'd love to hire someone, but with what we pay in rent for that space, we can't afford to bring anyone on. I'm barely making it right now as it is." What was with my impromptu honesty?

"Our lease ends soon. What if we found a different space? Something more affordable?"

"I'm open to that."

She merged onto the highway headed out of town. "And maybe you should consider renting out a room. That would help with your financial situation."

"She'll probably make me crazy, but maybe I'll ask Cami. She mentioned needing a roommate." I mustered up my courage for what I had to say next. "I spent the last two weeks furious with you and trying to figure out how to divvy up our business."

Haley stared at me, then snapped her head forward to look at the road. "Why? What happened?"

"I'm not mad anymore. At anyone. But I blamed you for what happened at the wedding. Aunt Joji booked every room so Hank and I had to stay together. You can imagine how I felt when I overheard her laughing about it at the front desk."

"I had no idea."

"I know that now, but I should have known that then. I'm sorry I didn't trust you."

Haley reached over and grabbed my hand. "Apology accepted. I did tell Aunt Joji I thought you and Hank should be together, as in, be a couple. Not meaning you needed to share a room. I guess that explains why Hank is walking around acting like his dog died."

Hearing that only made me feel worse. "I said some things."

"He told Zach."

"So you know."

She nodded.

I glanced up when she exited the highway. "Where are we going?"

"Lunch. And I want to show you a vacant space."

"In Stadtburg?"

She nodded. "If you don't want to see it, I understand. It's not close to our other location, but I saw it driving around. I thought I'd at least mention it."

"Let's see it." My plan to never set foot in this county again wasn't working out too well.

She turned into her favorite barbeque place.

"You want us to work in the back room of a barbeque joint?" I glanced around, hoping maybe Hank would make a surprise appearance. After all, he lived only a few blocks away.

In this town, almost everything was a few blocks away.

"No. Gosh, I wouldn't get anything done. I'd eat until I couldn't move." She pointed across the street. "That little shop is empty."

"Who do we have to call to get inside?"

"He's meeting us after lunch. His office is over there." She pointed at the end of the line of shops. "Convenient, huh?"

"Seems almost too good to be true."

CHAPTER 8

*T*wo days before Thanksgiving, I gave up boycotting my mother. I craved her cooking, and I didn't want to be alone for the holiday this year. As I approached the house, I scanned the street for Hank's truck.

Disappointment rattled in my chest when I pulled into the driveway without seeing any sign of him.

"Mama, it's me."

"In the kitchen!" She was almost always in that room.

She glanced up from her pie crust and waved her rolling pin. "You came back."

"I missed you." I dropped my purse in a chair and washed my hands. "How can I help?"

"The pecan pie recipe is on the counter. Start mixing those ingredients. I'll have this crust ready soon. I want to have enough pies to go around. You going to join us this year?"

"I'd like to. Will there be enough chairs?"

"Of course. I also invited Hank."

I washed my hands longer than necessary as I tried to

figure out what to say. "I'm surprised he isn't spending the holiday with Haley."

"She's going to her in-laws. Hank didn't want to get in the middle of that."

"That's sweet of him. It's good he has a place to be. Being alone on Thanksgiving isn't any fun."

"I invited you last year . . . and the year before that." She laid her perfectly round crust in the pie tin.

"I know. I'm sorry."

She turned around, her eyes wide. "We've missed you, *mijita*."

I nodded, trying my best not to cry. "We might need to make another one of these. Hank loves pecan pie."

"I have two already made. This one is for him to take home."

I snuck up behind Mama and wrapped her in a hug. "I love you."

"Aye! I love you too. So does he, but he thinks you were serious about it being over." She patted my cheek. "Go make his pie."

"Why? Is there magic in pecan pie?"

She waggled her finger, then dusted her hands on her apron. "Never underestimate the power of food."

"What do I need to eat to make me able to trust him?"

"Humble pie." Mama chuckled.

She wasn't going to make this easy on me.

~

I HELD THE DRESS IN FRONT OF ME, THEN MOVED IT TO THE side as I stared in the mirror. Which color looked better on me? I'd spent way too much time trying to decide what to wear. Why? I didn't want to admit the answer to myself.

Caring and trying not to care exhausted me.

Before walking out of the house, I turned up the sound on my phone. With the entire family together, there was no way I'd hear my phone vibrate.

At noon, I stepped through Mama's front door. Full of people, the house buzzed with laughter. Hank sat on the floor with my nephews as Ethan and Dylan toddled and danced. My sisters-in-law took advantage of the break and talked at the dining room table.

Facing Hank might be harder than I anticipated.

Just as I contemplated running back to my car, my brother Nico walked up and nearly tackled me. "Mama said you were coming, but I didn't believe her."

"Well, I'm here." I made the mistake of glancing toward the living room. "Did y'all drive in last night or this morning?"

Grinning, Nico watched his son Ethan. "This morning. Sam and crew flew in last night. I didn't want to overrun the house while Mama was trying to get everything ready." He nodded at Hank. "It's good to see him here. Are things . . .?"

"We're not together."

Hank glanced up at that moment, the hurt unmistakable.

"Uncle Hank." Four-year-old Dylan tapped his shoulder. "Catch me again."

"Sure, buddy." Hank wiggled his fingers, then crawled around while my nephew squealed and ran away.

"That's a shame." Nico patted my arm. "I'm disappointed to hear that. Come say hi. Everyone else is in the kitchen and dining room."

"It's not fair that you're making Hank babysit."

"He volunteered, and we ran." Nico laughed.

I stopped as Hank swung Dylan in a circle, then grabbed Ethan before he toppled over. "Hey."

Nico kept walking.

"If having me here is uncomfortable, I can go." Hank stood and shoved his hands in his pockets.

"No. I don't mind. Really. It's good to see you."

"Yeah." He stared at the carpet. "You look good."

"You aren't even looking at me." I tried to add a bit of humor.

It backfired.

He met my gaze. "You could be a thousand miles away, and when I closed my eyes, I'd be able to see you and remember every detail. You always look good."

Flustered, I opened my mouth, but no words came out.

Dylan tugged on my hand. "Aunt Nacha, you want him to chase you? He's fast."

"Yeah, Nacha, what he said." Hank grinned.

I hugged my nephew. "It's good to see you."

He wriggled free. "You go over there, and Uncle Hank can chase us. But you're big, so you need to get on the floor."

"Nacha, are you coming?" Sam, the baby of the family, leaned around the corner. "Nico thought maybe you'd changed your mind and left."

"I didn't leave." I gave Ethan a quick squeeze, then walked toward the kitchen. "We'll play later, okay?"

Dylan crossed his arms. "Promise?"

I nodded.

Why had I done that? Breaking a promise to a four-year-old kid was unacceptable, despicable even. Now I had to crawl around on the floor with Hank.

My brothers clapped when I walked into the kitchen. "She's alive."

"I missed y'all." I greeted everyone before looking around. "Where's Mama?"

Sam pointed down the hall. "Back there."

"I'll be back." I wandered back to her room. "Hi, everything okay?"

She wiped her eyes. "I'm fine, *mija*. Just missing Jeffrey. This was his favorite holiday."

"Because of the pie."

"Because being thankful was important to him. I should check the turkey." She smoothed her hair and wiped her eyes. "I don't want it to dry out."

"It's kind of nice having everyone together."

"It is. And thank you for coming and letting Hank be here too. Whatever happened with you, he'll always be family. I've told him that." She rubbed my back. "But he won't believe it until you act that way too. Thank you for that."

"He's in there playing with Dylan and Ethan. It's pretty cute."

She started down the hall. "Cute enough to make you change your mind?"

"I'm afraid to. What if we end up right back here again?"

Touching my cheek, she smiled. "And what if you don't?"

"I'll think about it." That wasn't a lie or a platitude. I'd been thinking about it every day since I said it was over, which made it seem like it was anything but over. "I promise."

What was with me and all my promises today?

~

STUFFED, I PUSHED MY PLATE ASIDE.

"You going to finish that?" Hank pointed at my half-eaten slice of pecan pie.

"There is an entire pie for you to take home. And there is still some on the counter."

"But why waste what's on your plate?"

I moved it toward him. "Help yourself."

"Thanks." He ate it like he hadn't had two other pieces.

The song "Come a Little Closer" rang out, and I glanced

at Hank. It was the first song we'd danced to, and when we were together, almost anytime it played, we'd stop what we were doing and dance.

Who was playing that song?

Hank nudged me. "Your phone is ringing."

I snatched it up and ran out of the room. "Hello?"

"Sorry to interrupt your dinner, but the Realtor just texted me. We got the place in Stadtburg. We can move in after December fifteenth." Haley's voice hummed with excitement.

"Good. That's great news. Monday, we should talk to Cami and see if she wants to answer phones."

Haley laughed. "She just can't ask customers if they're hot."

"Agreed! Enjoy the rest of your day. We're making sure Hank gets his fill. I think he's eaten half a pie."

"He loves your mom. I'm glad he got to be there today."

"Me too. Listen, I should get back to the kitchen. They'll think I'm shirking dish duty."

"See you Monday."

I crossed my arms and leaned against the wall. Every word of the song echoed in my head. It meant more now than it had when we first danced. My eyes slipped closed.

"Aunt Nacha?"

There was no such thing as peace and quiet with little ones around. "Yes, Dylan?"

"Are you ready to play chase? Grandma said you didn't have to do the dishes. I asked."

"Then I suppose it's time to play chase."

"Does suppose mean yes?"

I nodded.

"I'll get Uncle Hank." He bolted away.

Crawling around on the floor in a dress with Hank chasing me wasn't how I'd pictured my day.

I tucked my phone in my purse. When Hank stepped up next to me, I could feel him before I heard him. And the scent of his cologne teased me.

"Hey, I figured you would've noticed that I changed the ring tone before now. Sorry about that." Hank stood just a little too close.

Was it obvious to everyone that I'd been flustered? "It's fine."

"Which means it's not. And I'm sorry."

I smiled. "I'm okay. It just caught me by surprise. I rarely have my sound turned on."

"If you don't want to play, I don't mind tangling with them." He let his gaze slide downward. "You aren't exactly dressed for a game of tackle."

"I'm not breaking a promise to a four-year-old. I think that brings unlimited bad luck or something. *And* no one said anything about tackle. He said chase."

"What do you think happens when I catch you? The tackling part was implied."

"Just play nice."

He winked. "He's four. I'm not going to hurt him."

"I was talking about me."

Reaching up, he stopped before touching my face. "I never meant to."

Dylan jumped up and down. "Let's play." He crinkled his nose. "Ethan can't run. He's too little, but my daddy said he has to play too."

"Ethan and I will stick together." I dropped to my knees, and Ethan toddled toward me.

On all fours, Hank growled.

That set off a series of screams as Dylan ran away. Ethan giggled. I hoisted him onto my back and moved at a turtle's pace.

After chasing Dylan around the room two or three times, Hank caught him, unleashing a roar of giggles.

"Catch Aunt Nacha. She's too slow."

Hank headed toward me.

With Ethan clinging to my neck and hanging off my back, steering options were limited, and speed was impossible.

Next to me, Hank flipped to his back and tugged me on top of him, keeping Ethan safely off the floor. "Gotcha."

Dylan piled on, his infectious laugh drawing others into the room.

With my lips inches from Hank's, I inhaled.

The kids crawled on us, and it was like a glimpse of a possible future . . . one I was too scared to pursue.

Hank tugged at the hem of my dress. "There are things your brothers do *not* want to see."

Dylan clapped. "That's how Daddy tackles Mommy."

Sam swooped in and grabbed Dylan. "Nap time, buddy. After all that food and playing, you've got to be tired."

Nico roared with laughter, enjoying the fact that his kid was too young to talk.

Careful of my dress, I rolled off Hank, then stood up.

Hank handed Ethan to Nico, then glanced at the time. "I should probably head out. Thanks for having me. I've had a great time."

Mama pulled Hank into a tight hug. "You're my favorite son-in-law. Never forget that."

Considering he was her only son-in-law, being the favorite didn't seem like a huge compliment.

She ran out of the room, then came back with a tin-foiled-wrapped pie. "You'll always be one of my boys. Nacha and I made you a pie to take home."

"Thanks. I'll try to make it last until tomorrow." He yanked his keys out of his pocket. "Have a great evening." With a wave, he walked out the door.

Fear kept me from running after him. I hated being afraid of pain.

~

THAT NIGHT I PULLED THE DIVORCE PAPERS OUT. THE PAPERS I'd never signed and never turned in.

Even though I'd never told Hank that everything was final, he assumed it was. I knew that. But when I went before the judge, I couldn't end the marriage.

After so much time, I wasn't even sure how to bring it up. I needed to either get over my fear or set Hank free.

With the papers on the bed next to me, I cried myself to sleep.

CHAPTER 9

The next morning I didn't wake up with clarity, just a bad headache. But there were things to be done. No matter what I decided about Hank, changes needed to be made.

I stuffed the paperwork back into the drawer and headed to the kitchen.

After a few sips of coffee, I called Cami.

"Hello." She sounded as if I'd woken her up.

I shouldn't have called before eight. "I'm sorry. I didn't mean to wake you. I'll call back later."

"No. That's okay. What's up?"

"I've been thinking about you needing a roommate. I have space at my house if you'd like to move in." Maybe this was my way of moving on. Not being strapped at the end of the month would make being single easier.

"I'd totally pay you."

"Yes, I'd assumed that would be part of the deal. When you have time, we can discuss it."

"Let me grab a shower, then I'll head over. Thank you! This means so much." She ended the call.

Based on her excitement, I guessed we wouldn't be easing into the new arrangement. But I'd wait to mention the job at the office until Haley was around.

I made myself instant oatmeal and added more brown sugar than would be considered healthy. Most mornings I topped my oatmeal with berries. Today, I wanted comfort food.

No sooner had I tucked my bowl into the dishwasher, someone knocked. It had to be Cami.

"Coming!" I ran to the door.

Haley grinned. "Hey. Cami texted that she was headed over, so I grabbed doughnuts."

I pulled open the door. "Where's Zach?"

"Fishing." She dropped the box on the table. The part she'd left off was that he was fishing with Hank.

Why hadn't I remembered their day-after-Thanksgiving tradition?

"I offered Cami a room. She's all excited."

"Did you mention that we needed someone to answer phones?" She shrugged off her coat.

I shook my head. "Not yet. Wanted you to be around."

Haley pulled the door open when Cami stepped onto the porch. "Come on in."

"This'll be great. We can hang out all the time." Cami flung her arms open.

She made me feel old. Was ten years really that big an age gap?

Haley laughed. "Grab a doughnut."

"First I want to see the bedroom. You really don't mind?" Cami pointed down the hall.

"First door on the right. And you'd have that bathroom across the hall pretty much to yourself." I stayed a few paces behind her.

She stopped in front of the wall of photos. "Whoa! Haley, your brother is hot!"

I walked to the kitchen. That was not a conversation I wanted to hear.

Cami ran in, giggling. "I was teasing." She wrapped her arms around me. "I thought you'd roll your eyes and shake your head." Feigning a pout, she danced her eyebrows. "Forgive me?"

"Yes. Go look at the room."

Cami ran back down the hall.

Haley crossed her arms. "Are you sure you're up for this?"

"She needs a place. And I have more room than I need."

A few minutes later, Cami bounced back into the kitchen. "I hope we can figure out something because this place is perfect." She scanned the box, eyeing every doughnut before choosing one covered in sprinkles. "Why Hank?"

I nearly choked. "What do you mean?"

"I'm sure there's a long list of reasons why you aren't together but why did you marry him? Those are the stories I like to hear." She broke her doughnut in two, then nibbled on the larger half until both pieces were the same size. After that, she alternated taking bites out of each one.

Haley set mugs of coffee on the table. "Because sparks."

"Very funny." I remembered the electricity that tingled my skin when he dropped kisses on my neck. "I fell in love."

Cami's pinched brow transformed into a wide grin. "His last name is Sparks!"

"Why don't we talk about rent?" I sipped my second cup of coffee, thinking a third might be required.

"And a possible job." Haley dropped into a chair.

Cami dunked a doughnut in her coffee. "Seriously? With y'all?"

I found a lemon-filled doughnut, telling myself it could be

counted as a fruit serving. "It would only be part time until January. Once we move into the new space, we can bring you on full time. You'd be answering the phones and doing office work."

She wiped her eyes. "Thank you. And with you, I joke all the time, but I can be professional. I hope you know that."

Haley rubbed Cami's shoulder. "We were counting on that."

I grabbed a notepad. "Let's talk numbers."

We spent the next hour, figuring out the details of Cami's new life.

ALONE AGAIN, I EMPTIED EVERYTHING CAMI DIDN'T NEED OUT of the guest room, which was going to be her room starting tomorrow. She hadn't really planned ahead for her lease being up.

Thankfully, Cami wanted the dresser and bed. Those would have been hard to move by myself.

But I could barely walk through my office. It would take several hours to find homes for what I'd moved out of the guest room.

I snatched up the phone when it rang. I still hadn't changed the ringtone, and I hadn't turned off my sound. "Hello?"

"*Mijita*, come have dinner with us. I'm making enchiladas."

Piles covered the desk and sat on the floor in the office. Fighting the urge to stay home, I inhaled. "Um, I've been moving stuff around, but let me change. I'll be over soon."

"Thank you."

I could picture the look on Mama's face and knew my brothers were leaving in the morning. "I want to see everyone before they leave." That was true. I loved my family, but I didn't like the scrutiny, real or imagined.

"I'm proud of you." Mama's tone was soft.

Words like that were only going to make me cry, and I'd done enough of that. If she knew what I'd done, she wouldn't be proud.

Haley would probably hate me. I didn't even want to think about Hank's reaction.

"Be there in twenty minutes." After the weekend, I'd set things right. At least as best I could.

But tonight was about family. I wouldn't wall myself off any longer.

CHAPTER 10

Not yet adjusted to having a housemate, on Sunday evening I crawled in bed early to read. I'd just gotten to the moment when the hero decides he needs to fight for love when my phone rang.

Why hadn't I changed that ringtone?

"Hello?"

"Mija, I only have a minute because I watch my show at nine."

"Mom, you watch it on Netflix." I'd set that all up for her.

If it was possible to hear someone rolling their eyes, that was the sound she made. "Yes, but every night I watch it at nine. Anyway, Hank came by earlier to say goodbye to your brothers. He's such a fine man, Nacha." She paused, waiting for me to agree.

I kept quiet. Hopefully, the silence would shout that I didn't want to discuss it.

"Anyway, Hank mentioned that his neighbor—she writes romance novels, I think—has been coming over almost every day. Maybe he'll ask her out. He deserves to be happy. But I made him promise that he wouldn't forget me."

Words pounded in my head. "She what?"

"It would be so convenient. She's right there. I probably shouldn't have said anything, but I thought you'd want to know." Mama sighed. "It's nine. I'll talk to you later."

Tossing my phone aside, I scrambled out of bed. "I can't let him . . . date. I can't let him go." That was the more honest answer.

My walls weren't who needed to hear that.

I couldn't wait until after the weekend. I had to talk to Hank now. If he was talking about this woman to Mama, he must be serious.

Fearing I didn't have the courage to try again, I panicked at the thought of losing him. All my muddled thoughts solidified into one crystal clear point—I wanted Hank. I loved him, hurt and all.

Grabbing my coat and keys as I ran for the door, I tried to figure out what to say. Words bumped into each other in my head.

"Nacha?" Cami paused her show. "Are you okay? Because you don't have, you know, clothes on."

"I'm going to see Hank."

She clapped. "Go, Nacha. He'll love what you're wearing."

Hoping Cami was right, I climbed into the car. I made sure to keep my speed under the limit. Now was not when I wanted to be pulled over, especially since I'd run out of the house wearing my flimsy pajamas but no shoes. With my luck, Eli would pull me over, and I'd have to explain everything. I was tired of explaining to Eli.

Best not to be noticed. I cared more about getting to Hank's than making sure I was wearing real clothes.

I parked next to Hank's truck, wondering which neighbor was vying for his attention. I headed to the porch, dancing my way up the walkway, suddenly conscious of the cold.

After only a second of me pounding on the door, Hank

answered. His lack of a shirt would make it harder to focus ... on words.

"Hey, you okay?" He glanced down at my feet. "Come inside. What's up?"

Overheating from my racing emotions, I dropped my keys on the coffee table and started to take off my coat, then remembered what I was wearing.

"You're in your pajamas." He inched closer, grinning. "Did you miss me?"

I nodded. "Mama told me about your romance-writing neighbor and how she comes around a lot. And she told me you were going to ask her out."

"What?" He slipped his arms around me, chuckling. "That's not what I said."

I leaned my head on his chest, wishing I hadn't waited so long to be honest with him. Here in his arms was where I belonged. "She said how it was good because you lived so close, but I rushed over here because you can't. You can't for lots of reasons, but mostly because I love you."

His lips caught mine, then his hands cradled my face. I could quit talking now, but that would be wrong. Delaying a minute or two was not wrong at all.

I pressed in closer, sliding my hands up his chest and around his neck. "I've missed you so much."

Sighing, he rested his head on mine. "Yeah."

Sucking in a deep breath, I mustered the courage to be honest. I was risking this perfect reunion. "I haven't been—there is something I need to tell you."

He danced kisses along my jaw. "Mmmhmm?"

"We aren't divorced. That's another reason I didn't want you to date your neighbor. But when you left, my reaction was wrong. I should never have reacted like I did. I should have gone with you to Montana."

His entire body tensed. "What did you say?"

"I was wrong. I should've gone with you and let you pursue the job you'd always wanted." I rested my head on his chest, praying his muscles would relax.

He jerked away and crossed the room. "Not that part."

I knew he'd be hurt, but I hadn't expected anger. As a rule, Hank wasn't quick to lose his temper, but when he did get mad, the wrath was suffocating.

I crossed my arms, battling tears. "I never turned in the papers. I couldn't. We aren't divorced."

His pulse throbbed in his neck, and fire danced in his eyes. "I was crushed when I thought our marriage was over. And you let me believe it for over a year!"

"I'm sorry." My apology sounded small and shallow.

"You wouldn't even answer my calls. I've told everyone—I've filled out tax forms saying that I was single. I'm probably going to be audited." He jammed his hands in his pockets. "What if I'd met someone, Nacha? When did you plan to tell me?"

"Hank, in the beginning, I was so hurt, and then it had been so long, I wasn't sure how to bring it up."

He waved his hands. "I think this was perfect. Now I know that I need to file new papers. I need you to leave."

"No. We need to talk."

"That's gold coming from the woman who wouldn't answer my calls."

"I have a lot to apologize for." I wouldn't be able to keep my tears at bay for long, but I refused to let him think they were a form of manipulation.

He opened the front door and pointed outside.

"Please, Hank."

His icy gaze stabbed at my heart. "You said it was over."

"I didn't mean it." I wrapped my arms around his neck. "I want you, Hank. I miss you."

"Don't touch me."

I backed up. "What can I do to make it right?"

"Just go. Right now, I'm angry and can't talk to you. When this subsides and I can say your name without spitting it out like overcooked, boiled vegetables, then I'll call you. And when I do, you better answer." His jaw set, he stared at the ground.

I hated that I'd hurt him. Holding in my sobs, I ran to the car. What a horrible mess! And it was all my fault.

Sitting in the driveway, I wondered which house belonged to the stranger who was hitting on my husband. Had she seen me? Should I run around in my pajamas a little longer, so she'd know to stay away?

Knocking on doors to warn her off was probably—it was absolutely a bad idea.

I jolted out of my thoughts when Hank slammed the front door and turned off the porch light. I wasn't a moth. The light had nothing to do with why I was still here.

I tried to start the car but realized my keys were inside. I walked back to the door and knocked.

He didn't answer.

Again, I knocked, letting my coat hang open in case the neighbor was watching. I pressed in close to the door. "I left my keys."

The door opened, and he held out my keys. I couldn't even see his face.

Acting purely on impulse, I pressed a kiss to the palm of his hand before grabbing my keys.

He shut the door without saying anything.

If the neighbor saw all that, she was probably planning their first date.

Sobbing, I drove out of town. I'd made it almost to the highway when I had to fight for control of the car. Pieces of my tire bounced in the road behind me. Pulling off to the side, I reached for my phone . . . and remembered that it was still on my bed.

After waiting for ten minutes, I opened the car door. With so little traffic on this road, I could sit here for hours and not get any help. Walking along the side of the road barefoot in my pajamas would make people think I was drunk. But what other choice did I have?

I stepped out onto the pavement, then jumped back into the car. Maybe I'd just wait a few more minutes. It was downright cold.

Thirty minutes later, flashing lights appeared behind my car. I wiped my eyes and pulled my coat tighter as I rolled down my window.

Eli strode up. He pulled his hat off his head and dragged his fingers through his hair. "Oh, Nacha. You . . . uh . . . are you okay?"

Crying clearly made the man uncomfortable. And thanks to my track record, he probably thought I cried a lot. I didn't, but that didn't matter right now.

"No. Hank and I argued, then I had a flat. And my phone is at home."

He shined his flashlight into the car. "And you don't have shoes on."

"And I'm in pajamas. Could you please not tell anyone about this? I just want to call someone to fix my tire or tow my car. Whatever."

"How will you get home? I'm guessing you don't want me calling Hank."

"That wouldn't be a good idea." Barefoot and stranded in pajamas on a Sunday night, I was thankful for the few people I could call. "Will you call Haley for me?"

He nodded. "Good idea."

If Hank hadn't already shared the news, she'd come

rescue me. If he had, I might be stuck on the side of the road all night. And I probably deserved it.

THIRTY MINUTES LATER, AFTER DISCOVERING MY SPARE WAS also flat, my car was being loaded onto a tow truck.

Zach's Explorer pulled off to the shoulder, and one glimpse of Zach's face said he knew. He didn't get out of the SUV.

I inhaled as Haley walked toward me. "Thanks for coming to get me."

She crossed her arms. "You've got to be freezing. Get in."

"Did he tell you?" For all the years I'd spent caring about how things looked, now I cared about saving my friendship.

She nodded.

"Hank has every right to be mad. I should've said something ages ago. I'm sorry. Can you ever forgive me?"

Her lips pinched. "Probably, but not tonight."

I climbed into the backseat. "Thanks, Zach."

A quick bob of the head was his only answer.

During the silent car ride to my house, I determined to do all that was in my power to rebuild my friendship with Haley. And whatever it took, I'd make Hank see that I loved him . . . even if he decided it was really over.

The thought made me ill, and I slapped a hand over my mouth. Getting sick in Zach's car would not help the situation.

CHAPTER 11

Cami walked on eggshells all morning. Apparently, having my hair tied up in a knot and red puffy eyes gave off an unapproachable vibe.

After I'd finished my coffee, I broke the silence. "Can I get a ride to the office today?"

She nodded. "Uh-huh."

"You're probably wondering about last night." If I didn't let people in a little, I'd look like the ice queen.

"Forget last night." Cami cradled her mug. "I'm wondering about right now. You look terrible. And—no offense—that's not like you. I've never even seen you cry."

I swallowed back the urge to give her a snippy answer and reveal nothing about what happened. "Things didn't go well with Hank last night. Then I had a flat. And almost everyone I know is upset with me—albeit deservedly—because I let Hank think we were divorced for over a year." I pressed a hand to my stomach. "I think I'm going to be sick."

"Are you pregnant?" Cami slapped a hand to her chest.

I shook my head. "Didn't you hear me when I said *over a year*?"

"But you—I didn't know if . . . never mind. I'm sorry your life is in the toilet. You probably should've told him sooner."

"Yes. If I had, I wouldn't be in this mess, but I don't have a time machine." The conversation was giving me a headache, so I headed back to my room. "I'll be ready in about ten minutes."

"I think you'll need longer than that. But I don't mind waiting."

Why had I invited Cami to live here?

After checking the calendar, I yanked on jeans and Hank's t-shirt. I rarely wore jeans to the office, but I didn't have any client meetings today. And somehow wearing his shirt gave me a sliver of hope that I could win him back.

When I walked out to the living room, Cami jumped up. "Oh! You're just going with that look. Okay." She wrapped me in a hug. "You kinda look like you need one. On the way to work, we'll figure out what you should do."

"Cami, I appreciate your friendship, but I'm not sure the problem can be solved during a drive to work."

"Sure it can. We just need to find the right saying and use that as the plan." She locked the front door, and we headed for the car. "Is this an absence makes the heart grow fonder problem? Or is the way to a man's heart is through his stomach better advice?"

Mama's words played in my head. She made Hank all his favorite foods.

"Cami, you're a genius."

She beamed. "No one has ever said that to me before."

"I know what I'm going to do. I don't know if it will work, but it's at least a place to start." Having a plan loosened the grip on my heart. "But that doesn't help me know how to get Haley to forgive me."

"Maybe we should stop for coffee."

"Great idea. My treat." It was good I'd asked Cami to

move in when I had. I might be completely broke by the end of the month. And there were less than four weeks until Christmas.

I knew what I'd be asking Santa for.

Armed with coffee and doughnuts, Cami and I walked into the office. Haley's door was closed. But her car was out front.

"Put the stuff on the table. I need to talk to her." I shrugged off my coat.

Cami crossed her fingers. "Good luck." Her expression said what her mouth didn't: I'd need it.

I knocked and waited.

"Come in." Haley's' eyes were rimmed in red.

I squatted next to her chair. "I am so sorry. I never meant to deceive people. It just—I let myself be blinded by the sting of it all. And then I focused on how it all looked. Please forgive me."

Haley wiped her eyes and nodded. "You really love my brother?"

"More than I thought possible. And I've been so stubborn."

"Now he's being stubborn." Haley put her hand up. "Not to speak ill of your husband, but we both know that's one thing y'all have in common."

"True." I dared to hope my friend didn't hate me. "Are we okay?"

She threw her arms around me. "We need to figure out how to thaw Hank. He wants you too. He just needs to admit it." Pulling back, she wiped her eyes. "It won't be easy."

"I know. But—at first, I went over there because of blind jealousy. Mama told me about the neighbor who has been going over there a lot. That's why I ran out of the house in my pajamas. I couldn't stand the thought of him with someone else, but when I got to his door, I realized that

Hank is home for me. I miss him, and I miss me. I'm a better person with him in my life."

Haley giggled.

"I'm not sure what part of that was funny, but okay."

"The neighbor who shows up all the time is pushing seventy. I think she's totally sweet on Hank in a weird old lady kind of way."

"Mama set me up."

"It sounds like it."

"Our coffee is getting cold while we jabber. Come grab a doughnut." I stretched. "I think I'll spend part of the day packing."

"And I can take you to get your car later."

"Tonight, I need to go see Mama. I haven't told her yet, and I need her to teach me how to cook."

"Wow, you are serious about this."

"As serious as poison oak." I ran before Haley could swat me.

I found Mama on the back porch, sipping a margarita. "Bad day?" I asked.

"No. But I bought some limes, and then suddenly I was craving a margarita. Have a seat. Want one?"

"No thank you." I dropped into the brightly colored metal chair that used to sit on my grandparents' porch. Twisting my fingers into a knot, I tried to figure out where to start. "I messed up."

"I thought you'd never figure it out. I'm so glad. You and Hank are meant for each other."

"More than that."

Her eyes narrowed. "What did you do?"

That look from Mama did not make it easier to tell her. I hated disappointing her.

"I never turned in our divorce papers, so we're still married."

"Ay, Nacha." Shaking her head, she pressed a hand to her heart, then pulled in a long sip of her drink. "Does he know?"

"I told him. He's upset."

"How could you do that? What were you thinking?" She whispered something in Spanish that I didn't make out. "Keeping that secret was selfish."

"I know. I know." I yanked the scrunchie out of my hair and then pulled it back up into a tangled knot.

She tapped the side of her glass, which made it clear she was in strategy mode. "What are you going to do?"

"I don't know."

"I know. I don't know. You are all over the place." Mama waved her hand from side to side.

"I have one idea, but I need your help."

"Mija, I don't want to interfere. You and Hank need to work things out." That was gold coming from the woman who fed my jealousy.

"You have to teach me to cook his favorite foods. I don't even know what he likes to eat when he comes over here." The idea didn't sound as genius as it did in the car.

"But you don't cook!"

I leaned forward and grabbed her hand. "Please. You have to help me. You were the one who told me not to underestimate the power of food."

"You'll help me make tamales?"

I remembered how much work went into shredding the pork and assembling the tamales. Usually, my mom made them alone. I just gave them as gifts to close friends.

"Does he like them or are you just using the situation to get my help?"

Mama grinned. "He loves my tamales. Says they are the best he's ever had."

He had said that. Multiple times. He could down an entire dozen in a matter of minutes.

"This weekend?"

"Yes and the weekend after. Come over tomorrow, and I'll teach you to make *carne guisada*. He loves that with fresh tortillas."

"Will you teach me to make tortillas?"

That must not have been her plan because she sipped on that drink again. "I'll try."

"Thanks, Mama. Pray that this works."

She nodded. "And that you don't make him sick."

"Mama!"

Laughing, she stood. "I'm joking. You'll be great. And *buñuelos*. He loves those. And *polvorones*." She rubbed her belly. "I'm making myself hungry. Come on. You get your first lesson tonight."

Hoping there was magic in her kitchen, I paid close attention as we mixed cookie dough and rolled the pink-tinted dough balls in sugar. "I love these. You haven't made them in a while."

"Reminds me of Jeffrey. We met buying *polvorones*. Please don't mention that I bought them at the store. No one needs to know that."

"Of course not." I hid my smile.

"But I made them for Hank's birthday this year." She moved the last few to the cooling rack. "We'll pack these up and tomorrow, you can take Hank a snack. He's on shift."

"You want me to take them to the fire station?"

She patted my cheek. "That's exactly what I want."

I nodded. If it gave me any chance of winning Hank, I'd do it. "Thanks for helping me."

"Helping you? I want a granddaughter. Your brothers don't seem to be good at that."

"I'll see what I can do."

She giggled. "See what you can do. You're funny. Need me to explain it to you?"

"No, I don't!" I stacked the cookies into a plastic container. "No more margaritas for you."

Her smile fell away, and she rubbed my arm. "I'll pray, and we'll cook. He'll come around."

"I hope so."

"And then I'll pray some more."

Her confidence in a happy ending—more like the lack thereof—made me want to cry. Again.

I hated crying.

That night, before crawling into bed, I called Aunt Joji. The call rolled to voicemail, which was probably for the best. "Hi. This is Nacha. I'm not sure if you are back in San Antonio yet, but I wanted to check in with you. I'd love to hear your story, and . . . I'll fill you in on the rest when I see you." I ended the call and crawled into bed, wearing Hank's shirt. How many days could I wear it before getting disapproving looks from Cami and Haley?

I hadn't even finished fluffing my pillow when my phone rang. Hank's choice of ringtone played, and I fought tears again. "Hello."

"I'm so glad you called. I just arrived back in town today. Are you free tomorrow night?" Aunt Joji sounded as bubbly as ever. Clearly, she hadn't learned of my horrible selfishness.

"Yes. Just let me know where to meet you. I was going to get a cooking lesson from my mother, but I'll let her know I need to reschedule." Why was I telling all of this to Aunt Joji?

"Cooking lesson? I want to come." Was there anything the woman didn't attempt?

Mama loved having people in her kitchen. But I couldn't imagine two women more different than Mama and Aunt Joji. Seeing them together would be entertaining.

"Sure. I'll text you the address and meet you there about six. If that works."

"Perfect. Let me know what to bring."

Introducing Aunt Joji to my mother felt reckless and dangerous. But with both of them on my side, how could I lose my bid for rekindling love?

"I'm looking forward to seeing you again." I wasn't looking forward to telling her Hank hated me.

"And I'm looking forward to hearing *the rest*." Aunt Joji sighed. "Am I going to like the news?"

"No. Do you have a minute?"

"As many as you need."

Rather than making her wait, I told her what I'd done and how Hank had reacted.

She chuckled. "The two of you are quite the pair. So, um, the cooking lessons . . ."

"That's part of my plan for winning Hank back. It's all I know to do."

"It's a good start. The man does like to eat. See you tomorrow night." Aunt Joji hung up.

I slid under the covers and shot off one last text before turning off the light.

Hank, I'm sorry.

I didn't expect an answer. I just hoped he wouldn't block my number.

CHAPTER 12

Staying parked along the street outside the fire station was only going to draw attention. I needed to muster my courage and deliver the *polvorones*. The problem was, I hadn't figured out what to say.

Maybe I should've waited until he called me. Since he hadn't, he probably still thought my name tasted like overcooked, boiled veggies. What a description. He hated overcooked veggies.

If I went home without delivering the cookies, Mama would give me an earful. I glanced at the plastic tub full of sweets. Eating all the *polvorones* myself was an option. And I considered it. But then I'd have cookie crumbs and sugar all over my car.

Before I gave into my cowardice and cookie temptation, I pulled into the lot. The crew was outside, grilling and tossing horseshoes.

Aware that I was being watched, I smoothed my dress as I stepped out of the car. Not wanting to be the center of attention had to take a backseat to my desire to see Hank. If I showed up at his house, he might not even answer the door. But here? He couldn't pull his normal avoidance tactics—tactics I'd also mastered. And he was too much a gentleman to be rude to me even if he wasn't happy to see me.

I flashed my best smile and held up the container full of cookies. "Is Hank around? I brought him some goodies."

Some of the guys clapped.

A tall one, blonde and built, waved. "I hope he shares. Let me get him."

He stepped into the building, and Hank emerged a minute later. He wasn't as happy to see me as the other guys were.

Determined to keep my promise to my mother, I marched up to him. "I thought you might like some *polvorones*."

His gaze snapped to the container. "*You* made them?"

"Mama taught me. I thought you might like them."

"This doesn't make us right." Reaching to take them, he gave me the once over. "Thanks."

I caught his arm before he stepped away. "Mind if I bring you food again?"

"It's a free country. I'm sure the guys would love free food." He shrugged, staring at my fingers on his arm.

"You feel good." I gave his bicep a squeeze.

What I really meant was that I missed him. I missed touching him and kissing him. All his working out hadn't gone unnoticed. But I'd love him even without all those toned, hard muscles.

"Bye, Nacha." He popped the lid off and stuck a cookie in his mouth. He was probably trying to decide if he would share.

A guy with dark hair and even darker eyes ran over. "Hank, you going to introduce us to your . . ."

The complete lack of subtlety made me want to laugh. But I didn't.

"Nope." Hank turned and walked away.

I strolled to my car. Now he knew I was thinking about him, and I'd given the guys something to talk about. That was the best I could hope for on my first attempt.

The delivery had been made. I swung by the house and grabbed clothes before heading to Mama's. I stayed in my dress. Mama and Aunt Joji would appreciate seeing what I'd worn to deliver the cookies.

The unfamiliar car in the driveway had to be Aunt Joji's. Introducing her to Mama might be the biggest mistake of my life, but I needed all the help I could get.

"I made it. There was quite a bit of traffic coming back from Stadtburg."

Mama wiped her hands on her apron as she walked into the living room. "Look at you!"

"Aren't you all fancy? That dress fits you *very* well." Aunt Joji popped her hands on her hips. "Was that the idea?"

"We made cookies last night. I delivered them to Hank at the station."

Aunt Joji tossed her head back and laughed. "I am impressed. Josefina, your daughter has spunk."

"She knows what she wants." Mama smiled and pointed to the kitchen. "Let's get started. I'm already hungry, and we haven't even started cooking."

Aunt Joji rubbed her hands together. "I can't wait."

"Let me change. I may need this dress again." I walked to the guest bedroom.

After pulling on jeans and a t-shirt, I stared into the mirror. There was no easy remedy for what I'd done. I wouldn't win Hank back with a few well-seasoned dishes. But I couldn't give up.

I made sure my ringer was turned on and set on the highest volume. If he called, I'd answer. No matter what.

When I walked into the kitchen, I checked my texts. Hank hadn't even said if he liked the cookies.

I tapped out a quick text and sent it to him. *I keep thinking about how good it felt to be snuggled on your side of the bed.*

The man had the nerve to reply with a thumbs up.

"He's so stubborn." I set my phone on the counter.

Mama and Aunt Joji laughed. "Pot meet kettle."

"I know. I know. Show me what to do." I pointed at the beef. "We're making carne guisada, right?"

"Yes. You can start by cubing that into small pieces." Mama filled three glasses with iced tea.

Aunt Joji watched over my shoulder. "All day, I've been thinking about how to help you without getting in the middle of things."

"I'm open to ideas." Thinking back to Haley's wedding, and all the mistakes I'd made, all the chances I'd given up, I shook my head. "I just hope I didn't wait too long. I'm not sure how . . ." Crying into the food would be gross. I blinked away my tears. "I really need to figure out what will work."

"I mentioned to Haley that we needed to get together as a family more often. It's only the three of us left. And you and Zach." Aunt Joji turned to Mama. "And Josefina, you are always welcome at any of these family gatherings."

"I'll remember that."

"Anyway, what if we all gathered for Christmas?" She patted my shoulder. "We could go back to the resort."

Sitting in front of a crackling fire and snuggling against Hank sounded like the perfect way to spend the holiday. "That's a great idea. Check with Haley, and if that works for them, I'm all in."

Christmas with Hank would be the best gift ever, but that wouldn't give him much time to get past the hurt. And I knew—because I was a master at nursing my pain—hurt could last a long time.

"I'll have to let Haley talk to Hank. He's still not taking my calls." She waved a hand. "That man doesn't know who to be angry with."

Once the meat was simmering on the stove, Mama took over and showed us how to make Spanish rice. "The meat has to cook for over an hour. I figured we'd be hungry, so I made a batch earlier." She lifted the lid off a pan on the back burner. "When the rice is ready in fifteen minutes, we'll eat."

"That's why it already smells so good in here." Aunt Joji inhaled. "Just divine."

I hugged Mama. "Tastes even better."

I'd been spoiled growing up with such a great cook as a mother.

We all settled around the table, our plates full of food. "Aunt Joji, I'd love to hear your story. Especially the part about being just like me."

She laughed. "So many years ago. But yes. Once upon a time I met my prince. His name was Oscar. He stole my heart, and he wanted to marry me. But instead of holding down a regular job, he tinkered with stuff in his garage and worked a side job to cover the bills. I was afraid that to others he seemed lazy. And they would think I was stupid for marrying him, so I held off giving him an answer. My heart and my head didn't agree."

I dropped my tortilla and leaned forward. "What happened?"

"That man had the audacity to die before I could answer him." She wiped at a tear. "And in his will, he'd left everything to me."

"That's terrible." Mama jumped up and grabbed a box of tissues.

"And those things he tinkered with . . . the patents ended up making a whole lot of money. It's how I can travel and book entire resorts. I was so worried it would look like he couldn't take care of me, and he's taken care of me all these years."

"It's hard to imagine you worrying about what people think." I dabbed a tissue to my eyes. "Do you want me to take the leftovers to Hank?" I gathered the dishes.

"No, dear. Give him a few days. No calls. No texts. No food." Mama looked at Aunt Joji. "Do you agree?"

"Absolutely. Give him time to miss you. I'm guessing all the guys he works with will be talking about the cookies, so you'll be on his mind. And I'll call Haley tomorrow and ask her about Christmas."

I hugged them both. "Thank you. For the cooking lesson. And for helping me."

THE NEXT NIGHT I MADE THE SAME THING, BUT WITH MAMA looking over my shoulder.

"You need to be able to make it without me around. He needs to know that *you* cooked it."

"Are you going to make me make this every night this week?"

"Not tomorrow. Joji and I have plans. You can practice at home."

"I'll make more cookies. Where are y'all going?"

"Out. Maybe dancing." She wiped the counter and didn't look up.

I replayed her words in my head. "Did you say *dancing*?"

"We'll be listening to music. I don't know if anyone will ask me to dance. If it goes well, we may go out on Thursday also."

"Have I created a monster?" I couldn't remember the last time she'd gone out for fun.

To her, the grocery store was entertainment.
Mama smiled. "I made a new friend. And she's fun!"
"Aunt Joji is that."

CHAPTER 13

Friday night, I made carne guisada—again—while Mama and Aunt Joji sipped margaritas and recounted their adventures from last night.

"Then tall, dark, and handsome strolls up and tips his hat to your mother, and she giggles. Oh my. He loved that. Then he asked her to dance, and she left me alone most of the night." Aunt Joji turned to face Mama. "What time is he picking you up tomorrow?"

My mother's cheeks turned a fiery red. "Seven. Dinner and dancing."

"I'm a wee bit jealous. Maybe one day, I'll find my own cowboy." Aunt Joji took a bite of food. "Nacha, this is wonderful."

"Thank you. I plan to cook it again tomorrow for Cami, just to make sure I can consistently get it to taste good."

Mama nodded. "I have no doubt. This is perfect."

I sat down at the table, amused by the quick friendship that had bloomed. "Aunt Joji, between your lack of shoes and the suitcases sitting in the guest room, I'm guessing you aren't staying at the hotel anymore."

"Why would she? I have plenty of room." Mama grinned. "Having her around makes me feel young again."

Aunt Joji lifted her glass. "Hear, hear. I feel the same way."

Even if I didn't feel like laughing, it was nice to be around happy people. Grumpiness didn't have a chance to survive around Aunt Joji. And Mama's kitchen was the epitome of comfort.

As the evening continued, Aunt Joji shared stories from her travels.

My thoughts drifted to the tickets for Madrid. The dates were set for late spring. Would I need to change the reservations? Was there any possibility Hank and I would go there for our second honeymoon?

I'd passed the cooking test for one dish—two if you counted the rice. I still had so much to do. And Hank hadn't called.

While the new best friends giggled and jabbered about plans for tomorrow night, I cleaned the kitchen. Seeing Mama so happy warmed my heart. Hopefully, my brothers wouldn't be bothered by her dating again.

SATURDAY NIGHT, I THOUGHT ABOUT MAMA WHILE I MADE carne guisada and Spanish rice. She was so excited about her date. I hoped her date would go well. It was an odd feeling being nervous about my mama's love life.

I lifted the lid on the rice and smiled. The texture was perfect. "Cami, you are in for a treat!"

"I can't wait. You've talked about it so much. I can't believe you're making it again."

"I wanted to be sure I could do it without my Mama around." I set plates on the table.

Cami jumped up when the doorbell rang. "I'll get it. You expecting anyone?"

"Nope. And it's late for a door-to-door salesman."

"Exciting." She grinned and ran out of the kitchen. "Oh, hi! Nacha, there's a hottie at the door. He looks like the guy in the pictures hanging in the hallway."

"Be there in a few." I hurried to my room. If I'd had any inkling Hank would show up at the door, I wouldn't have been wearing a ratty, baggy sweatshirt.

My leggings would have to do. But I yanked his t-shirt over my head and pulled the clip out of my hair.

Cami chatted away, but I couldn't make out her words until I opened my bedroom door.

"You can wait inside. I don't bite. Not hard at least."

His expression must've been funny because she giggled.

"No thanks. I'm good out here." His voice warned me that stoic Hank had shown up.

Was he here because he couldn't live without me and wanted me back? Padding down the hall, I tried not to get my hopes up. But why else would he have come?

One glimpse at his expression dashed any glimmer of hope.

Cami backed away. "I'll just . . . let y'all talk."

I motioned him inside, but he shook his head. I stepped out onto the porch.

He eyed the shirt. "Did you go put that on just now so I'd see you wearing my shirt?"

"Yes. I changed clothes and let my hair down. Unfortunately, I didn't have time for a bubble bath and makeup."

"Very funny. Where's your mom?" He leaned around me, peeking through the open door. If he wanted to know who was inside, why did he insist on staying on the porch?

"She's not here. In fact, she's on a date." I crossed my arms to keep from wrapping them around his neck. Being so close and not touching him was a form of torture—one I'd made him endure.

"Quit teasing me. The house smells incredible. I know she's here."

I'd never been happier that one, I'd cooked, and two, I'd left the door open. "I'm the one who cooked. Mama went out."

His eyes narrowed. "You're serious? You and Aunt Joji aren't pranking me?"

"No prank." I inched closer.

"But it's Saturday." He scratched his head. "What was Aunt Joji doing at your mom's anyway?"

"I introduced them. They became fast friends, and Aunt Joji is staying there now. I'm thinking about calling them the *dangerous duo*. They even went dancing the other night. That's where Mama met her date."

He clenched his jaw and inhaled. "And you are just *letting* her go out with some guy she met in a dance hall?"

Not touching him wasn't working. I didn't have that kind of willpower. I pressed a hand to his chest. "Hank, she went out with a retired police detective. Aunt Joji met him. And Mama is a smart woman. Besides that, I'm not her mother. She's mine."

"What if she doesn't make it home?"

"Aunt Joji will call me. Heck, she probably tagged him with a tracking device."

Hank cracked a small smile. "She would, huh?"

"Mama will be fine. I haven't seen her so excited in a long time."

He glanced down at my hand. "All right, then. Sorry to bother you."

"It's sweet that you were concerned. Did you go over there tonight?"

"Bought some seeds and wanted to show her. I won't

plant them until early spring, though."

This man had no idea how hard it was not to tackle him.

I loved that he did those things for Mama. "Would you like to stay and eat? I made carne guisada."

He shook his head, then pointed inside. "Who's visiting you?"

"Cami? She lives here. I rented her a room." I kept my hand in place, hoping he wouldn't back away.

"Why would you do that?"

I tamped down the urge to tell him to mind his own business. Admitting things that made me feel like a failure were difficult. Having him upset with me only highlighted my failures. "Things were tight. I didn't want to lose the house."

His brow furrowed and he reached out but stopped short of touching me. Then he stuck his hands in his pockets, and his expression became unreadable. "I'm not sure what I think of her."

"I know what she thinks of you."

He rolled his eyes and stepped backward. "The whole neighborhood does."

"Want to take food with you?" I hated the distance he put between us.

"Sure."

"Hank, I—"

"Let's not talk about any of that. I'm not ready." He stared at the ground. "It still stings. But I'll call you at some point."

"And I'll answer." I'd felt that way for so long, I understood completely. "Let me get you food."

"And keep Cami—or whatever her name is—inside. Please. The last thing I need is both of you coming on to me."

I closed the distance between us and wrapped my arms around his waist.

He tensed. "Nacha."

"If you think what I was doing before was coming on to

you, you haven't seen anything. Would you like me to show you?"

"Please don't. Your stunt at the station caused me enough trouble."

I grinned and walked to the door. "Maybe I'll stop by again. Give me a sec to get the food."

Before I made it all the way to the kitchen, Cami threw her hands wide. "I've been waiting. Tell me what's going on. Y'all were standing where I couldn't see crap looking out the window."

"I'm getting him some food to take with him. He was worried about my mother."

"That was his *excuse* for stopping by."

"I wish. He still doesn't want me to touch him. Not a good sign."

She served herself food. "Give him time. It took you over a year." Cami had a real knack for pointing out what didn't need spotlighting.

"Thanks so much for the reminder. I'd completely forgotten about that." I hoped my sarcasm was obvious. I loaded two containers with food, then hurried back outside. "Here. And you're welcome to stop by anytime. If Cami makes you uncomfortable, I can go to your house."

"We'll see." He walked back to the truck.

I didn't have to ask how someone who was so in love and so passionate could be so cold. I'd spent a year letting anger and the sting of perceived rejection hold me captive.

Hank needed time. I could give him that, but I wouldn't give up on him.

At least he hadn't brought up the topic of divorce papers. And he took food with him. I'd mark those two things as wins.

But the only win that really mattered was winning back his heart.

CHAPTER 14

Sunday afternoon I rolled out tortillas, struggling to get them to resemble a circle.

The whole time, Mama gave me the replay of her date. "He was so polite. And he can dance. It's like floating on a cloud."

"Are you going to go out with him again? Where's the griddle?" I opened a couple of cabinets.

"The *comal* is next to the sink."

I turned on the burner and let the *comal* heat.

"He invited me to dinner on Friday." She picked up the rolling pin and rolled out a perfect circle.

"And?"

"I said yes."

I dropped a tortilla onto the hot *comal*. "I love seeing you so happy."

"I never planned to date again. Never. I haven't even mentioned it to your brothers."

"They won't mind. They want you to be happy."

"After a few dates, I'd like for you to meet Mateo. Hank too. Joji mentioned that he stopped by."

"He came to my house, looking for you. He thought you were there because it smelled like your cooking."

Mama smiled. "Did you give him any?"

"I did."

"What did he think?"

I shrugged. "I haven't heard anything. Waiting is hard. I know he needs time, but I want him back."

She flipped the tortilla on the *comal*. "Patience. Keep showing him you love him."

"I plan to."

"Hellooooo!" Aunt Joji filled a room before she even made it through the doorway.

"Hi! Mama said you had lunch with Haley."

"I did. And now I have good news and bad news. Which do you want first?" She picked up a hot tortilla and dropped into a chair. "Oh! Hank is gonna love these."

"Good news, I guess."

"Hank joined us for lunch. I think being mad at me *and* you is just too much for the poor guy." Her laughter echoed through the house. She sighed. "And the bad news. Christmas won't work. Hank is working that day."

"Oh." I'd pinned so much hope on spending Christmas with him.

"But everyone agreed that a family getaway is a good idea. Let me know what dates you're free. I'll book the resort again." Aunt Joji turned to Mama. "You can come too."

"We'll see what's going on then." Mama continued rolling perfectly round tortillas.

"What that means is that she's not sure if she'll be busy dating Mateo." Aunt Joji picked up another tortilla. "I could eat my weight in these."

That would probably be achieved by eating three.

"Christmas is only two weeks away." I needed to figure

out what to get Hank. It had to be memorable and make an impression. But I didn't have a big budget.

Mama filled glasses with sweet tea. "The rest of this week, we'll make tamales."

"I need to give Hank more than tamales."

Aunt Joji pushed a card across the table. "I'm giving you your gift early. In case you need it."

"You don't have to—" I stopped talking when she put up one finger.

She lifted her chin and stared me down. "Are you rejecting my gift?"

"No." I hugged her. "Thank you."

I hadn't mentioned my financial situation to Aunt Joji. What had Hank and Haley told her?

Aunt Joji drank down half her glass of tea. "I think we have extra help."

Mama laughed. "We need all the help we can get."

"What do you mean?" I burned my fingertips, trying to flip a tortilla without using tongs.

"Haley is clearly in your corner. She plays it cool, but that Zach. I like that man. He turns to Hank at dinner and asks if —" She glanced at my phone. "Hank just messaged you."

I grabbed my cell, chiding myself that I forgot to turn on the ringer. I closed my eyes a second before reading the text Hank sent: *The food was good.* It had all the warmth of a forced thank you at Christmas, like when my least favorite aunt gave me a training bra as a gift. Mama gave me that look, and I said my proper thank you. But who gives that as Christmas gift? To an eight-year-old?

I replied: *I'll make it for you any time.*

That stupid thumb appeared again. I was beginning to hate that little emoji.

"You were saying something about Zach." I pulled the tortilla off the *comal* and dropped another on.

Mama shook her head. "Not before you tell us what he said."

"He said the food was good. That's it." I slathered a pat of butter onto a hot tortilla, then took a bite. "That's all he said."

"Back to Zach." Aunt Joji added butter to her tortilla. "Oh! This is even better. Anyway, Zach leans over and asks Hank what he thought of the carne guisada. Right at the table where we can all hear."

I thought back to Zach's comment the night I fell into the pool. I should've given Hank more of a chance then. But it was good to know Zach wasn't playing favorites.

"Let me guess, he said it was good. Did I get that right?"

"Nacha, he raved about it. Said that—Josefina, I'm just repeating what he said—it was even better than your mom's."

That couldn't be true, but why would he say that? He had to know it would get back to me.

"I know it isn't, but I'm glad he liked it."

"Keep at it. It's working." Mama clapped. "Tomorrow we start on the tamales. I'll cook the pork tonight."

That night, alone in my room, I opened Aunt Joji's card. A gift card fell onto the bed, but before picking it up, I read the card. She'd scrawled a couple of sweet lines about wanting me happy and back together with Hank.

I picked up the gift card and gasped. Five hundred dollars! With that kind of money, I could get Hank something really nice. Now I just had to figure out what to get. I needed something that Hank would love and something that said, 'I want you.' Maybe getting him two gifts was a better way to handle that.

Cami sang out my name. "Nacha, I'm home."

"Hey. Good day?"

She shrugged. "Haley said the pics were good. That author lady seemed happy. I just wish she wanted covers with couples on them. Maybe I could meet some nice, hot model dude."

"Maybe we'll have another author book our services. Then you might need to pose for pics with a guy." I thought about Hank's neighbor and cringed at the idea of her asking Hank to pose for a cover shoot. Thoughts like that would land me in jail. And I really didn't need to add that to my list.

Cami crossed her fingers. "Here's hoping. But earlier today, I did find some good stuff. My Christmas shopping is almost done."

"I still have to shop for Hank. What do you get a guy that doesn't want to be around you?"

"Something awesome *and* something sexy. Like something only you'd see—you know—if you get back together. I mean *when*." She danced her eyebrows. "What does he do besides workout? That part is obvious."

"He's my husband, Cami."

"I'm not trying to steal him. I'm just saying."

I pictured Hank flopped on the sofa with a game controller in his hand. We'd spent so many weekends together on the couch when we were dating and first married. He played games while I read or edited photos. Did he still do that?

"Thanks. You've given me an idea." Since I'd be making tamales tomorrow night, I'd have to sneak out of the office to get the something awesome. "See you in the morning."

Tucked in bed, I scanned shopping sites, looking for the perfect gift. Would he even open what I gave him? I'd have to think of a plan for that too.

When my eyes burned from exhaustion, I snapped the laptop closed and slid under the covers. It was after midnight, much later than I used to stay up. Sleep and I weren't on the best terms. Sleep came and went on its own schedule, leaving me awake many nights.

When "Come a Little Closer" rang out, I answered before the end of the first ring. "Hello."

"This is how this will work. I'll ask a question. You answer. There is a lot we need to talk about, and I'm not promising that we can patch things up."

"Thank you for calling, but wouldn't having this conversation in person be better?"

"No. It's this or texting."

"The phone is fine."

Hank shuffled. "I'm trying not to make the same mistakes we made before by not communicating. But seeing you physically hurts right now."

I wouldn't be stopping by the fire station for a while. Causing him pain was the last thing I wanted to do. "Ask me anything."

"After I told you over and over that being apart was short term, you reacted like . . . like I'd run away with someone else. Why? I want to understand." Clearly, he didn't believe in throwing softballs.

"Hank, I—" I swallowed, hoping the emotion choking me wouldn't erupt into sobs.

"I don't know isn't an acceptable answer. Honesty is the only hope of finding a way through this . . . if one even exists."

"I've never talked much about my father."

"Jeffrey? You've talked about him." Hank didn't make this easy, but at least he was talking to me.

"Not Jeffrey, my biological father. His name was Eric. He left when I was three." I pulled the covers up to my chin, feeling very exposed. "I don't really remember him. But I do remember Mama crying at night in her room. When I was old enough to notice that most kids had a mom and a dad, I thought more about how I didn't have one—a dad. And I thought it was my fault. Maybe I was a horrible kid and he couldn't take it. Maybe he wanted a boy. Whatever the reason, he left. And it made my mama cry."

The only sound coming over the line was Hank breathing in and out. He hadn't hung up on me yet.

This part was harder to say than the rest. "When you packed your bags and left, I couldn't hear your words. I felt like that little girl whose daddy walked away and never looked back. And I reacted with all the logic of a three-year-old. Can you ever forgive me?"

"Thanks for answering." He ended the call, probably battling emotion and not wanting me to hear it in his voice.

I knew all about the strategy for acting like life was wrapped up in a pretty package. And I also knew it didn't work.

CHAPTER 15

The next few evenings were spent at Mama's house. I spread *masa* on corn husks, and she added seasoned pork to the center, then folded the tamales into shape. Between that and work, my hands stayed busy. My mind was always on Hank.

He hadn't called again, but when I slept, the phone was always by my pillow.

"I'm out of masa." I dropped my spreader on the table and stretched my back.

Mama counted the tamales stacked on the sheet pan. "Five dozen. This is a good place to stop. The batch in the pot is almost done. I may cook one more batch before I go to bed."

"Let me help you clean up." I checked my phone before tucking it in my pocket.

"Have you talked to him?" Mama hadn't asked about Hank in days.

"Not for a few days. I'm concerned it's too late to make things work, but until he tells me that, I'm going to keep trying."

She rinsed bowls and tucked them into the dishwasher. "Have you explained why you were so hurt? He'd want to know."

"A little." Telling Mama about his late-night call was more than I wanted to get into tonight. The conversation felt private and personal. I hadn't told anyone that he'd called. "When are you and Mateo going out again?"

"Day after tomorrow. Hank is coming over tomorrow night." She grinned. "So if you want to forget your coat or something..."

"I may drop by, but I won't stay."

Her eyes twinkled with mischief. "I need to run to the store. Will you come by and be here in case I don't make it home in time?"

"You mean, so that when you don't make it home in time, I'll be here to sit awkwardly with Hank."

"Exactly. And don't you dare let that man wait in his truck."

I sighed, picturing him doing exactly that. "I'll do my best."

"Oh, and if you'll make rice. That would be good too." Mama wiped off the table. "That clean-up went faster than expected."

I wrapped her in a hug. "Thank you for teaching me all this and for trying to help me."

She cupped my cheek. "I didn't know you carried so much hurt about Eric. I'm sorry I didn't tell you the whole story earlier. But I was taught not to speak ill of the dead, and..." She shrugged.

"He's dead?" Every time I thought I was fine with the situation, more information popped up that rattled me.

Mama laughed. "To me. I'm sure he's out there somewhere, betraying someone else and making their life miserable. But I don't have to think about that anymore."

Did I care if he was alive? I hadn't thought about meeting him in years. As a child, I dreamed of having him come back because he missed me. It was always about me. I wanted to be the reason he came back because I'd always thought I was the reason he left.

I blinked away tears. I didn't need to admit it out loud. Mama would tell me what I knew in my head. What Eric did was all about Eric.

I'd blamed Hank for moving away to take the job because I'd made it all about me. His dreams didn't even factor into my thoughts. How could I have been so wrong?

She tapped my hand. "Hank is a good man, Nacha. The very best. And he loves you. When he went fishing with your brothers this summer, he told them the same thing."

"They did what?"

She drew out her words. "They. Went. Fishing. You know, with poles and worms or whatever they used to feed those fish. That's all they did—feed them. No one actually caught anything."

"So . . . all of you hang out with Hank more than I do?"

She grinned. "Yes, but we're trying to change that. It would make life much less awkward. You should go. It's almost nine. I want to watch my show."

Arguing and explaining about streaming wasn't worth my time. "See you tomorrow."

"You'll see Hank tomorrow. Wear something . . ."

That was great advice. I'd be sure to wear something. Although maybe the alternative would get a better reaction.

"I'm sure you'll pick something he likes." She hugged me again. "I love you, and he does too."

Somehow those words made me feel better. I'd just keep reminding myself of that.

I'd checked the clock way too many times to count. The hot pan sat on the stove, waiting for me to start the rice. If I added spices to the pan, Hank would show up right after, and I'd probably burn the garlic. That wouldn't smell good.

I waited, watching the second hand move around the clock which had hung on Mama's wall for years.

Since she took my car to the store, Hank would be surprised to see me.

I fingered the buttons on my dress, remembering when I'd worn it on our honeymoon. He'd taken his time undoing each button. I didn't need to think about that right now, but hopefully he would when he saw me wearing this.

I ran to the door when I heard his truck but waited for him to knock. "Hey, come on in. Mama should be back from the store soon."

His gaze traced every button down the front of my dress. "I'll just—"

"She said she better not find you waiting in the truck." I motioned him inside. "I won't tackle you."

He cracked a smile. "Where's Aunt Joji?"

"Out shopping. She's been doing that a lot."

"Christmas is her favorite sport." He shoved his hands in his pockets. "I still can't believe she's hanging out with your mom. Speaking of your mom, she's not going out with that guy again, is she?"

"Tomorrow night. Come on into the kitchen. I need to make the rice."

"This I've got to see."

"Hey! I cook."

He stood close as I drizzled oil in the pan. "Sweetheart, you slid pre-made food into the oven. Other than that, you lived off oatmeal and salad kits. But don't mistake that for complaining." How could he act mad and flirt all at the same time?

I toasted the rice in the pan and leaned back only a little. My back rested against his chest. If I let my thoughts chase that rabbit trail, I'd burn the rice for sure.

He didn't back away.

That small lack of movement had my heart soaring. "What can I do to help you forgive me?"

He sighed. "We have more questions to tackle. Not sure there is anything more you can do. Even when you don't randomly show up at work or answer your mom's door, you're always on my mind."

"We do have a lot to talk about."

He nodded. "And that dress is the reason we're talking over the phone." After grabbing a drink out of the fridge, he stood next to me. "Show me how to make the rice."

I continued through the steps, explaining as I went.

Maybe Christmas would be merry after all.

CHAPTER 16

Christmas Eve I worked down my list. If I was going to be at Mama's on time, I needed to hurry.

I shot off a text to Hank. *Would it be okay if I dropped off tamales and rice? Christmas Eve isn't the same without those.*

He sent the dreaded thumbs up.

I'll be there about four. I'd added another deadline to my day.

I walked down the hall and froze.

Cami piled two months' worth of luggage near the door.

"Are you moving out?" I liked having her around more than I thought I would.

She shook her head. "No, but I never know what Mother and Daddy will have planned. One year on the day after Christmas, we had mimosas at the country club. Another year, we spent the day in the boat on the lake. So, I take a lot with me when I go home. But I'm coming back. Living here is too much fun." Cami didn't talk much about her family, but her money struggles didn't seem to extend to her parents.

"Good to hear. We'd miss you." I picked up a bag. "I can

help you load. If you don't leave soon, you'll be on the road all night."

She grabbed two other bags. "Traffic will be a nightmare, but it's less time at home. I can live with that." She grinned. "Just don't ever tell my parents I said that. I love them. I just love them more when they are two hundred miles away."

"Be careful driving. We need you back in one piece." While she stashed her laptop in the backseat, I nestled her present into the trunk.

"I left your gift on the kitchen table. And a little something for you to use when making your delivery." She threw her arms around me. "I hope the hottie forgives you. I'd have to move out then, but even still . . . I want y'all back together."

"Thanks. See you in a few days."

"Eight days. I'm coming home in eight days." She sighed. "See ya later." With that, she dropped behind the wheel, waved, and backed out of the driveway.

I ran back inside. Cami's gift, a small note, and a Santa hat lay on the kitchen table. Giggling, I knew why she'd given me the hat even before reading the note, but reading it confirmed my thought.

Wear this when you give Hank the gift. It'll guarantee a smile. And he'll know you aren't afraid to embarrass yourself to win him back.

Had I been that walled off that people thought I'd be embarrassed to wear a Santa hat?

The hat went into my purse. Wearing it was a must. Then I gathered packages, making sure I had everything I needed before driving to Stadtburg. Even though the town was only thirty minutes down the road, I didn't have time to drive there twice today and make it to Mama's tamale dinner on time. This year, I wouldn't miss time with family, unless it meant more time with Hank.

Haley's tamales went into the front seat. I'd given her

extra this year because of Zach. I guessed he could make two dozen disappear without a second thought.

Hank's gift—both parts—were placed in the trunk.

I ran back to the kitchen, pulled the foil pans out of the oven and carried them out to the car. Hopefully if my gifts weren't enough, the tamales and rice would be the way to Hank's heart.

When I arrived at Haley's, I could feel my blood pressure rising. Being away from Hank hurt more now. And getting him expensive gifts, which I was only able to justify because of Aunt Joji's generous gift, showed him a vulnerability I hadn't risked in over a year.

"Hiya. Come on in." Haley's gaze dropped to the box in my hand. "You really got Hank an Xbox?"

"I did. And tell Zach how much I appreciate him setting it up at Hank's place. I'm hoping he will be surprised."

Haley laughed. "Oh, Hank will for sure be surprised."

"As I mentioned on the phone, I need to unpack the box because I'm going to use it to pack the other part of his gift."

"Now I'm intrigued."

"With things like they are, I wasn't sure if Hank would open a gift from me. But—"

"If the other guys see Xbox on the box, he'll open it. And be surprised." She laughed. "Brilliant."

I tried to picture the look on Hank's face. Hurt was the only thing there. "Hang on."

I ran to the trunk and grabbed the gift bag holding the fun stuff I planned to shove into the console box. "Will you put this under his tree for me?"

"He doesn't have a tree, but I'll make sure he gets it." Haley squeezed my arm. "At least he isn't acting like life is normal and good."

"I never meant to hurt him, and watching him in pain is heart-wrenching.

Haley nodded. "Want to come in for a few minutes?"

"No, I need to run." I hugged Haley. "Everyone is gathering at Mama's, and I don't want to be late."

"What's in the bag? Is that what you were going to put in the box that formerly held the Xbox?"

"Please don't peek. I don't feel right about giving it to him at the station. Maybe I shouldn't give it to him at all." I picked up the bag. "I'll save it for later."

"Nacha, are you okay?" Haley touched my arm.

"I will be. It's so hard trying to figure out how to let him know I love him without depriving him of the space and time he needs."

"Curiosity is going to kill me. And now I have to wait longer before I'll know what you got him."

Hopefully, my smile covered my nervousness. "I definitely took a risk with this one. But I'll give it to him . . . one day."

She pulled me into a tight hug. "I'm rooting for you. We all are."

"I know." I waved and ran to my car. "Merry Christmas. Enjoy the tamales. I helped make them."

"I can't wait! Tell Cami to be safe on the road and to have an awesome Christmas."

"She just left, but I told her." I started the engine and headed to the station. Counting did nothing to calm my nerves.

The guys were outside again, and this time, Hank was with them. He noticed my car as soon as I pulled in the lot and walked toward my car. Another guy—it might have been the same dark-haired guy from last time—walked along beside Hank.

"Merry Christmas." I flashed my best smile.

"Nice hat." Hank glanced over his shoulder at our company, then rolled his eyes.

"Cami gave it to me."

"Figures." He crossed his arms.

That meant he wasn't going to hug me.

The dark-haired guy stuck out his hand. "I'm Mitchell."

"Nacha. Nice to meet you."

Hank pointed at the car. "Floorboard or trunk?"

"Trunk. You might need to heat stuff a little. But it was hot when I left." I didn't mention the short detour.

Mitchell looked from me to Hank. "So, um, is she . . . yours?"

I bit back a smile and turned to watch Hank answer.

He sucked in a deep breath, his gaze locked to mine. "Women aren't property, Mitchell."

Hank was a master of avoidance.

I crossed my arms and walked toward the trunk. "It's complicated."

Hank stayed right behind me and groaned, then lowered his voice. "Our love life is none of his business."

At least Hank and I agreed on one thing.

"Mitchell, mind carrying this inside?" I opened the trunk.

"Let him carry the rice. He'll eat all the tamales before I have a chance to get any." Hank picked up the tamale pan.

"Hank, I have a few more dozen for you at my house." I handed the rice to Mitchell.

Grinning, Mitchell walked toward the building, calling out, "The food is here, guys!"

Hank stayed near the car. "More tamales?"

"More of anything you want." I leaned in close. "I left your gift with Haley."

He turned, his lips inches from mine. "I didn't expect—we didn't talk about exchanging gifts."

"You don't have to get me anything."

He pinched his lips together. "I've been talking to a friend of mine. What we had was good. But I'm not sure we can get past our distrust and hurt. There's been a lot of hurt, Nacha."

Tears stung my eyes, and I turned so he wouldn't see them. "I'm not ready to give up on us, Hank."

He shrugged. "I haven't made up my mind."

"Your friend—what's her name?"

It was the wrong thing to say, and I knew it even before I let the words tumble out.

"Great example of the distrust problem." He marched away.

With my back to the building, I dabbed a tissue to my eyes. How had I ended up in tears? In a Santa hat no less?

I needed to get in my car and leave, but being able to see was an important part of driving. I dropped into the front seat, frantically trying to stop the incessant flow of tears.

Someone knocked on the window.

I pushed the button to lower it.

Hank scrubbed his face. "I should've kept my mouth shut."

"Me too." I opened the door and stepped out of the car.

"I hate that you're crying." He stared at the ground. "And that I didn't get you anything."

I kissed his cheek. "I love you. I hope your shift is quiet."

He hugged me. "Merry Christmas."

That alone felt like a Christmas miracle. "You too."

I wiped my face. Giving into tears felt like giving up. I wasn't ready to do that. Yes, I had trust issues, and between us we had enough hurt to break up a hundred marriages, but none of that outweighed the most important thing—we belonged together. He brought out the best in me. And I did the same for him.

I climbed into the car and drove to Mama's.

CHAPTER 17

*T*hat evening, Hank called Mama. She beamed and waved me closer. "Merry Christmas to you too."

I sat next to her, not expecting that he'd want to talk to me.

"Thank you. I'm glad you liked them. Nacha helped me this year. She could probably make them without me now."

That wasn't true.

"Would you like to talk to her? She's right here." Mama's smile drooped. "Oh." Then her face lit up. "Here." She pushed the phone toward me. "He wants to talk to you."

Hank had to know he was being tag teamed.

I put the phone to my ear as I walked out of the room. "Hello?"

"Your mom sounded disappointed that I didn't want to talk to you. So I figured I'd say howdy." He cleared his throat. "That sounded awful. I didn't mean . . ."

"Don't worry about it. I get it."

"I don't really have anything else to say. I'll let you get back to your family." He groaned as alarms sounded. "Talk to you later."

"Love you." I wasn't sure if he even heard me because the call ended in the middle of the last word.

So much for wishing he'd have a quiet night.

I handed Mama her phone. "Thanks. He had to leave on a call."

"I wasn't sure who it was until Mama handed you the phone. I thought for a minute it was her boyfriend. But I think he's a secret." Nico shot a glance at Sam, the tease in their look unmistakable.

Mama paled. "I was planning to tell you after the kids were in bed. He isn't a secret."

Inside, I fumed. There was only one way my brothers knew about it if Mama hadn't told them. Hank would get an earful.

"She told me all about him. He sounds nice, and I can't wait to meet him." I glared at my brothers who would not stop snickering.

Mama stood. "I invited him over for Christmas dinner." She walked out of the room, leaving us all stunned.

"That part I didn't know." I yanked out my phone, then tucked it away. I'd rather yell at Hank in person. Besides, he was out on a call.

Nico and Sam looked contrite.

Sam hesitated before walking down the hall. "We were just being funny. I think it's great that she's dating."

"Maybe you should tell her that." I gathered my stuff. "I'm going to go, but I'll be back in the morning."

Mama fanned her face as I walked into the kitchen. "I should have told them sooner, but I didn't know how. And Mateo is coming tomorrow."

I hugged her. "That's great."

"I invited Hank too. That's why we're eating a bit later than normal. He has to work, but I'm hoping that when he gets off, he'll come over. I know he wants to meet Teo."

"It's Teo now?" I was eager to see Hank, but focusing on the nickname Mama dropped was easier to talk about.

Mama blushed. "That's what I call him."

"I'll be here early, so I don't miss anything. Love you."

She patted my cheek. "I hope Hank comes tomorrow."

"Me too." I had my own reasons for wanting to see him.

∽

Christmas morning at Mama's was a flurry of wrapping paper and laughter. I'd dragged myself out of bed early to be there when the littles woke up to open presents. It was totally worth the loss of sleep.

I stuffed paper into a trash bag while my brothers played with the new toys . . . and the kids. Everyone else was in the kitchen, getting the meal ready. Our special guest was arriving soon, and Mama's cheeks grew redder by the minute.

A very exhausted Hank arrived first, and I happened to spot him before he made it to the porch. Yes, because I was standing near the window and watching the driveway. I ran out to meet him.

"Your mom invited me." He looked nervous.

I'd had way too much time to fume about him telling my brothers about Mateo. "How dare you!"

He put his hands up. "If you don't want me to stay for Christmas dinner, just say so."

I poked at his chest. "You called my brothers and told them about Mateo."

"Yeah, I did." He clasped my hand and held it against his chest. "Since they don't live around here, I promised your brothers I'd look out for you and your mom. That was back when we were dating. But I aim to keep that promise. No matter what happens with us."

Stunned, I wasn't sure if I should give in to my anger or my awe. "But why call them? She was going to tell them."

"I'm sure she was, but I let them know that I'd been asking around. Even though I hadn't met the guy, he seemed okay."

"Did you have Zach run his name?"

"No." Hank dropped my hand and rubbed the back of his neck. "He wouldn't do it. I just asked around."

I wanted to rant at him and tell him he didn't need to look out for me, but after having him rescue me from a pool, that declaration would only sound silly. Besides, I liked the idea of him looking out for me.

"I had no idea you made that promise."

"Promise or no promise, I'll always do it."

"Always?" I inched closer, hoping for a tiny crack in his hard-shell exterior.

"We should go inside. It would look weird if Mateo showed up and caught us out here talking." He spun around and headed to the door.

"Be nice to that man." I ran to catch up with Hank.

"I'm always nice."

When Hank walked out of Mama's house that evening, my dreams of ringing in the new year in his arms faded.

I followed him out to the truck. "Thank you for coming. I know it meant a lot to her."

"I wanted to meet the new guy."

"I'm hoping my brothers warm up to the idea of Mama dating. They weren't rude, but I think their cool reaction has Mama worried. Thank you for making Mateo feel welcome."

"I like him, and I think he cares about your mom. Your brothers will come around."

"It was good to see you."

He nodded. "It's probably time for another question."

"Any time, day or night."

He opened the door and put one foot inside. "Text me when you get home."

"I will."

Twenty minutes later, I'd said my goodbyes and was on my way home.

I didn't speed, but I didn't drive like a grandma either. While trying to get the key in the door, I texted Hank. *I'm home.*

Had he even made it all the way back to Stadtburg?

Waiting for him to call, I propped my phone on the nightstand and unbuttoned my dress. The phone rang, and I swiped the screen before taking off my dress. "Hi. How was the drive back?"

I put my dress on a hanger, then hung it in the closet. Aware that he was quiet, I asked, "Are you there?" I unsnapped my bra.

"Oh, I'm here. But I'm thinking the video chat option was . . . more than I bargained for."

I slapped the phone face down on the table. "Give me a second to put something on."

"You do that."

I yanked his t-shirt over my head before picking up the phone. "I just swiped. I had no idea."

"Yeah, well, merry Christmas to me. Okay, so the question —why didn't you answer my calls?"

"Don't mistake this for a complaint, but these questions make me feel very exposed."

"You already gave me the visual for that."

"I'm trying to be serious."

"So am I. That's what I'll see every time I—all the time.

But I get it." He carried the phone around the house and out the back door. "Whenever you're ready."

I wasn't. This was a question for which I didn't have anything resembling a good answer. "Are you really putting in a pool?"

"Yep. See." He flipped the camera and showed the stakes marking the pool's footprint. "They'll start digging next week."

His decision to put in a pool made it seem like he was moving on without me. He knew how terrified I was of the water. That was selfish thinking, and I had done plenty of that. Instead, I tried to imagine how he'd look stepping out of the pool, dripping wet.

"Hello?" He tapped the screen.

"It looks great."

"I'm excited. Now back to the question."

I snuggled under the covers, wishing he were next to me but glad I could see his face. "I don't have a good answer for that question. I was mad, and I wanted you to know that. So I didn't answer. But it was stupid because I cried every time I dismissed your calls. But seeing you hurting now makes me regret every single phone call I ignored. I don't like causing you pain."

He inhaled and blew it out. "I should have camped on the porch and made you talk to me."

"I won't blame you for what I did wrong."

"Thank you for that. I have my own regrets though." He looked away, and for a minute, everything was quiet. "I won't ask any other questions tonight."

"I love you, Hank."

"I know." The call ended.

Instead of feeling gutted, I laid the phone next to my head and closed my eyes. We'd found the path, but it would take a lot of steps down that road before we'd be back together.

I chose to focus on the steps.

CHAPTER 18

*T*he next few days were full of family, friends, and laughter, but no texts or calls from Hank.

I stretched out in a lounge chair on Zach's porch. Now that they were married, I referred to their place as Haley's house, but this would always be Zach's porch.

He plucked out Christmas songs on his guitar as Haley and I sipped hot chocolate.

"Hank has been working like a crazy man. We've hardly seen him." She flashed a wide grin. "Your gift was awesome. He loved the Xbox." She pointed inside. "And I saved the box for you. In case you needed it for a future gift."

"You mean like a Valentine's Day or an anniversary gift?"

"Exactly like that."

"Thanks." I wasn't sure when I'd give him the satin sheets and silk lingerie, but I would when the time was right.

Zach stopped playing. "Hank was irritated with some guy named Mitchell—"

"That's the one who asked if I was Hank's."

"He didn't!" Haley's jaw dropped open.

Zach's expression made us both laugh. "Apparently he

went on and on about the tamales. I just hope the guy has the sense not to ask you out, Nacha. Hank would pound the man."

"If Mitchell can't figure out that I'm sweet on Hank, the guy needs help."

Haley sighed. "Have you talked to him?"

"A little."

She leaned forward. "Please tell me what you bought. I'm dying to know."

Zach played another Christmas song. "She has no patience."

Haley pointed toward the house. "Can I bribe it out of you with a Moon Pie?"

"No, thanks. I've had enough sweets to last me the rest of the year." I grinned. "When I give it to him, he'll probably mention it."

"I might not live that long. It's killing me I tell you. Did you get to meet your mom's new boyfriend?"

"We did. He came over for Christmas dinner. He seems really nice. And Hank behaved himself. Thankfully."

"I wondered about that. He hadn't said anything."

I finished the last of my hot chocolate. "I should go. I'll never stay up until midnight tomorrow if I don't sleep tonight."

"You are coming tomorrow, right?"

"I'll be here. Cami is jealous. She wants to come too. I tried to talk her out of driving in crazy traffic to get here." I shrugged. "But who knows?"

"Harper will be here. So will Eli. Cami would be in heaven." Haley rolled out of her chair. "I'm glad you came over tonight."

"This was fun. Thanks for inviting me."

Zach waved. "You're welcome anytime."

After staying awake way too late, wondering about Hank's silence, I slept until noon. Waking up rested was blissful. I warmed tamales, then filled a mug with coffee. A glutton for punishment, I grabbed the photo album from our honeymoon.

This would not help me be productive, but I didn't care.

Flipping through pages, I relived each day. Money had been tight. The photography business had been tiny back then, but Hank had surprised me with plane tickets to Colorado. We'd spent most of the week snuggled in a mountain cabin, but the little town with all the shops was someplace I'd never forget.

Memories toppled over each other, and I moved the cup so my tears didn't land in my coffee.

Before I lost my nerve, I sent Hank a text: *I'm sitting here, looking at the album from our honeymoon. I miss you.*

I waited for that stupid thumbs up to appear.

Instead, a happy face popped up. No words. But that was progress, right? At least we'd moved up from that dreaded thumb.

That gave me a small glimmer of hope that he'd show up at Haley's tonight.

She'd offered me the guest room, so after I finished my breakfast—I guess it was technically brunch—I tucked a few things into a bag. Ringing in the new year with one of those drinks Hank had gotten me at the wedding meant I wouldn't be driving after, so I packed to stay the night.

The house was so quiet without Cami. I waffled about whether to text her. As much as I wanted her to be at the party, I knew how bad the roads could be on New Year's Eve.

She solved my conundrum. *Hey, I'm not going to make it. Daddy planned out my whole evening. Oodles of joy.* I thought *about leaving as soon as dinner was over, but now I have lunch plans tomorrow with some stuffy suit, his partner's nephew, or something—definitely not of the hero variety. Happy New Year!*

I shot back a quick text. *Don't fall head over heels for him. We miss you.*

Of course you do! She followed her text with a happy face.

I was getting a lot of those today.

Hours later, fueled by that happy face, I knocked on Haley's door.

Giggling sounded from inside. "Put me down. I need to get the door."

"I'll help." Zach's tone held a hefty dose of teasing.

The door opened, and Haley's feet greeted me. Flipped over Zach's shoulder, she craned her neck, trying to see me. "Hi there."

"I can come back later if you need some time alone." I enjoyed giving them a hard time.

Zach grinned. "Come on in. Aunt Joji should be here in a few minutes." He squirmed as Haley reached down and tickled his side. "Everyone else is out on the patio." He set Haley on her feet and smirked. "An eye for an eye and a tickle for a tickle."

She wriggled as if he were touching her. "Not now. Please."

"I don't even have to touch her. It's very entertaining." He tugged at the end of a curl. "I should check the snacks and make sure the guys haven't eaten everything."

Haley watched him walk out of the room. "Let's get you settled in the guest room. I'm glad you decided to stay the night."

I bit my tongue, forcing myself not to ask about Hank. If he showed, great. If he didn't, I'd still enjoy myself.

We walked into the bedroom, and I dropped my bag on the bed. "Thank you."

"I didn't want you leaving at nine to be home before the traffic got wild. You don't need to be by yourself tonight."

"I'm doing okay, Haley. Really."

For the first time in more than a year, the words were true. Things weren't perfect. But no matter how it ended with Hank, I felt okay.

I hugged her. "Thank you for being such a great friend."

"Thanks for being such a great sister." Haley jumped up when someone knocked. "That must be Aunt Joji. We invited your mom too."

"She has plans with Mateo."

Haley pulled open the front door, and Aunt Joji sashayed in. "Is everyone ready to have a good time? I brought us a bottle of wine." She handed me my favorite Spanish wine. "In case anyone didn't want to toast the new year with champagne."

"Thanks. He told you?"

She winked. "He did."

I set the wine in the kitchen, then joined everyone else on the patio.

Zach made the introductions. "Aunt Joji, I think you met everyone at the wedding. But here's a refresher. That's Eve. Attached to her is Adam. Harper, unattached. And Eli, also unattached."

She hugged each person. "So nice to see all of you again. She pointed at Harper's drink. "Where can I get one of those?"

"Coming right up." Zach laughed as he walked into the house.

Despite the urge to retreat into the chair farthest from the group, I pulled it closer to Aunt Joji. "It's good to see you."

"You too, dearie. Did you talk to your mom?"

I accepted a drink from Zach. "Thank you."

He hadn't asked what I wanted, but magically it was my new favorite mixed drink. For someone who was being scarce, Hank sure made sure all my needs were met.

I turned back to Aunt Joji. "Yes. She sounded so excited. I'm glad I introduced the two of you."

"I'm having a blast."

"We missed you at Christmas. The next time you want to free up space at Mama's, you can stay at my house. It's not big, but I'll make room." The idea of Cami and Aunt Joji in the same house amused me.

She patted my hand. "I'll keep that in mind."

Dancing flames in the fire pit kept back the chill of the night air. I leaned back in my chair and listened as Harper told about his recent blind date.

"So, I let Eve's mom set me up. That was a mistake, and I blame all of you." Harper pointed at Adam and Eve. "Especially you two."

Adam laughed. "How bad could it be?"

I'd heard about Adam's bad blind date and couldn't wait to hear Harper's story.

"It wasn't that she was bad looking or anything. But she showed up wearing a flannel dress. That just made me think of pajamas. But that wasn't the issue. I don't have anything against flannel. The real issue was that conversation consisted of me asking a question and her giving one-word answers."

Eli leaned forward. "She was probably just a little shy."

Harper rolled his eyes. "I figured that out, thanks."

"Nothing wrong with a girl who's a little shy." Eli flopped back in his chair.

"If I can find her number, maybe I'll introduce you. I need someone with a little more spunk. Personal preference."

Haley shot me a glance, and her thoughts might as well have been painted on her face.

"Would you go on another blind date if someone else set you up?" I sipped my drink, determined to make it last a while.

Harper shook his head. "Nope. I'm done with blind dates. I'm going to find someone who calls me a superhero without going on any more blind dates." He pointed at Haley. "I see you looking at Nacha. Whatever you're scheming, don't."

She laughed. "Okay. I'll let you find your own sweetheart."

"Thank you." Harper tossed a stick into the fire and watched it burn. "Someone else can tell a story now."

The evening continued, and I enjoyed every minute. Shedding my guarded shell was more freeing than I'd expected. How had I let myself get so closed off?

When I stepped inside to fill my plate, Aunt Joji walked in with me.

She shot a conspiratorial glance over her shoulder. "Now that we're alone, I can tell you. I talked to Haley and Hank about a family getaway."

"Oh?"

Noises came from the kitchen, and she stepped closer. "Hank said the earliest he could do it was April, and that even then, he'd try to make it, but I told him that if he canceled on me, I'd invite that guy—oh, what's his name?"

Zach leaned in from the kitchen, chuckling. "Mitchell."

"Yes!" Aunt Joji grinned. "Hank didn't think it was funny. But he'll come. I just know it. I'm sorry it's such a long wait."

"That's perfect. Just let me know which weekend in April works for everyone." Disappointment vied with anticipation in my chest. "I'm excited." And a little bummed that we'd have to wait so long.

Hank knew Aunt Joji would push us together.

She rubbed my arm. "I just wish it were sooner."

I reminded myself of the path. Hank and I were talking. That was more than we were doing a year ago, and for that, I had him to thank.

Minutes before the stroke of midnight, we all gathered with our drink of choice in hand and counted down.

As everyone was toasting the new year, my phone buzzed in my pocket. The message from Hank gave me hope that this year would be better than the last.

One little happy face appeared on my screen. I sent a heart in response, happy we were communicating . . . even if tonight it was only in emojis.

CHAPTER 19

Getting back into the rhythm of work after the holidays required an extra cup of coffee every morning.

For a week, Cami spent almost all day on the phone, and Haley and I were still answering calls on the other line. It was great for business, but it was exhausting. The calendar filled up, which gave me something else to think about other than the fact that Hank hadn't texted or called in three weeks.

Wasn't it time for another question? This time I'd be dressed before swiping to answer. Or maybe not.

Early on Saturday morning, I finished rinsing shampoo out of my hair when a text sounded. Leaving the water running, I jumped out to check. Trying not to land on my bare butt, I tiptoed to the phone.

Hank had messaged: *You dressed?*

With wet fingers, I replied hurriedly. *Just stepped out of the shower, but give me two minutes, and I will be.*

A video chat request popped up a second later but disappeared before I could swipe to answer.

Another text from Hank popped up: *Kidding. I'll call soon.*

Shaving my legs would have to wait. And right now, no one cared or noticed anyway.

I pulled on a tank top and shorts and ran into the kitchen to grab coffee. My phone came with me. When Hank sent the video chat request, I was snuggled in my bed, fueled by half the cup.

"Morning. Sorry I interrupted your shower." He didn't have a shirt on, which completely made my morning.

Playing coy wasn't in my playbook. "I will interrupt anything I'm doing to talk to you, Hank. Anything."

"I guess I don't have to worry about you seeing anyone else."

"I'm only flashing one person these days, and that wasn't even on purpose."

He grinned. "Do you prefer this to a regular call?"

"It's nice to see your face . . . and your chest. I miss you."

"You miss me or my chest?" He quirked an eyebrow.

The teasing and humor that bounced between us reminded me of our dating days. It made me miss Hank even more.

"You. Definitely you."

His lips pulled into a tight line. "Question time."

"I'm ready." The flirty warm-up was a nice addition to the pointed questions. But it was the serious part that was growing us closer.

"Why didn't you turn in the papers?"

I bit my lip to stop it from quivering. The question dropped me back into the courtroom, and all the feels and regret from that day flooded over me again. "I went to the scheduled court date. And I had the papers with me. You'd signed them, but I hadn't been able to do that. I thought that in the courtroom in front of the judge, I would be able to finalize everything."

His arms folded across his chest, he held my gaze.

"But I started crying when I talked to the judge. We went into chambers, or whatever it's called, and he asked me about the situation. After I unloaded the whole story, he suggested that maybe I wasn't ready to sever our relationship. So I left. I can't tell you how many times I picked up the phone to call you. I wish I had."

"We've seen each other since then, and you didn't even drop a hint."

"After a few months passed, I wasn't sure how to bring it up. Hi, remember those papers you signed? I filed them away and didn't do anything with them. It sounded so stupid."

"It does sound stupid. I can't argue with you on that point." His brow furrowed. "I'll talk to you later."

"Wait. May I ask you a question?"

"You can ask. I might not answer." Even through the phone, his tightened muscles were noticeable.

"What happened in Montana? Why did you move back?" I didn't go on about how that opportunity was his long-time dream, but that made me even more curious.

He dragged his fingers through his hair. "Even before the divorce papers were served, I was thinking about coming home. Being away from you—even though we'd only been married a short time—was hard. So hard. But then I got those papers." He paused and clenched his jaw.

I pinched my lips, trying not to cry.

"I couldn't focus, and that's not the kind of job you can do without giving it your full attention. So after a few weeks, I explained to my boss that I couldn't stay." Hank inhaled, then let the breath out slowly. "I thought I'd run back, and you'd be thrilled to have me home. My heart broke a little more with every call you ignored."

"Hank, I'm sorry."

"No. I'm sorry. I'm sorry that I didn't camp on your front

porch and make you talk to me. We should have talked about all of this then."

I nodded.

"I'm not sorry I came home." He chuckled. "Can you imagine if I'd been gone for months and then came home to find Haley and Zach together? I might not have handled that well."

"You didn't handle it well when you were here." I was happy to end the call on a lighter note.

"I need to run. I'll talk to you later."

"Bye." After ending the call, I walked back into the kitchen and poured myself a second cup of coffee.

Our anniversary was in two weeks. Would I hear from him before then? Would the day pass without any acknowledgment?

Should I wrap up the satin sheets and lingerie and give them to him for our anniversary?

I STARED AT THE WRAPPED BOX, TRYING TO DECIDE IF I SHOULD give it to him this weekend or next. I didn't want to push him, but I did want him to know how much I missed him.

My skills in the kitchen continued to improve, and I could make all of Hank's favorites. I hadn't taken food to the station since Christmas. It was time.

Mama kept me posted on Hank's work schedule.

On Friday evening, what would have been my second anniversary, I chased Cami out of the kitchen. "The enchiladas aren't for you. Stop trying to sneak a plate."

"Can I at least go with you to the fire station? I mean—hello—that's where hero types hang out, right?"

"No way." I didn't want her anywhere near the fire station. I'd have to drag her away by her hair.

Once the food was packed up, I threw on my fitted jeans and a tight sweater.

I drove to the fire station, a little nervous about this visit. Instead of ringing the bell, I texted Hank. *I'm outside. I brought two pans of enchiladas.*

He replied right away. *Rice and beans?*

I was glad I'd made the extra effort to cook the sides too. *Yes, rice and beans too.*

Be right out. His text popped up as the door swung open.

I shoved my hands into my back pockets, hoping he'd give me a reason to pull them out. "Hi."

"Bringing me dinner tonight isn't a coincidence, is it?"

"I couldn't let the day pass without seeing you." It had been more than two months since I'd told him the truth, and this was the hardest day yet.

He rubbed my shoulder. "I've been thinking about you."

"Do you have any questions for me?"

"I don't want the food to get cold, but there is one I want to ask you. Can I call you later?"

"Always." I opened the trunk. "I bought these bags. I can stack multiple pans in each. Just give it back to me whenever you have a chance."

"Thanks." He lifted the two bags out of the trunk. "Happy Anniversary, Nacha."

"You too, Hank." I watched him walk into the station before climbing into the car. The trip home felt long.

Cami was pouting in the kitchen when I got home. "I had to go get takeout. I'm sure it doesn't taste nearly as good as your food."

"Thank you, and I'm sorry. I'll make you something tomorrow night." I started down the hall.

She jumped up and ran in front of me. "Aren't you going to tell me what he said?"

"He didn't say much. But he might call me later."

She hugged me. "That's awesome. If he's calling you, that's great news."

I still hadn't told anyone about Hank's questions. And if I wasn't careful now, Cami would find out. "We'll see. I'm just glad he's still talking to me."

I crawled in bed and read until the phone beeped. I read his text over and over.

Will you go to marriage counseling with me?

The idea of sitting in front of a stranger and airing our dirty laundry made me extremely uncomfortable, but it wasn't an unreasonable request. For Hank, I'd do almost anything. Except it wasn't just for Hank. It was for us. I loved that thought.

I didn't want him to assume a delay was hesitation, so I replied quickly. *Yes.*

Thank you. I'll be in touch. He wanted to work to save our marriage, and that knowledge was the best gift I could've gotten today.

I sent a kiss emoji before turning off the light. Maybe tonight, I'd be able to sleep.

CHAPTER 20

J'd arrived early because traffic wasn't that bad. And I spent the extra ten minutes sitting in my car, trying to convince myself not to hyperventilate. Besides Hank and Mama, no one knew how I felt about my father leaving. That information would be fair game in counseling.

But this wasn't just about me. Shining a light on my dysfunction was the best hope of survival for my marriage. *My marriage.* Thinking those words, I climbed out of the car and bumped into Hank's chest.

He caught me by the shoulders. "I wondered if you were ever going to get out of the car."

"Oh, hi. I didn't see you there." I wanted to lean into him and have him whisper that it wouldn't be so bad. But it would be bad. I knew it. "I wasn't going to stay in the car. I'm eager to work through our issues."

He clasped my hand and started down the sidewalk toward the main doors. "You look like you're about to hightail out of here."

"I'm a little nervous."

The glass doors opened, and he didn't let go of my hand. "You aren't the only one."

I expected that I'd have a week or more to prepare for this, but he'd snagged an appointment for Tuesday. Maybe not having so much time to think about how painful it would be to rip off the bandage would help.

I hadn't convinced myself that was true. "How did you get the appointment so quickly? I was surprised since you called yesterday."

He pressed the button for the elevator. "Tandy is a retired sex therapist. She referred me to a friend of hers."

Jealousy clawed at my throat. When had I devolved into a green-eyed monster? Trying not to let that show, I asked sweetly, "Tandy?"

He tugged me into the elevator before answering. "My neighbor."

The elevator doors closed, blocking my retreat.

I refused to look like a jealous fool because of an old lady who liked gawking at my husband. "Oh."

The office was right outside the elevator.

He pulled open the wooden door and let go of my hand. "Trust me, okay?"

"That's the reason I'm still here. And, you know, because the elevator doors closed before I could slip out."

He didn't laugh, and that worried me even more.

The point of marriage counseling was to focus on our relationship and discover what needed to be mended. Tips for how to mend the broken parts would also be helpful. But I sat in the waiting area wondering what the lady at the desk thought of Hank and me. He still had a firm grasp on my hand, but that was probably because he feared I'd run if he let go. I wouldn't.

Did she score couples in her head, setting odds for if they'd make it?

The office door opened, and a woman old enough to be Hank's neighbor abruptly stopped my wondering. "Please, come in."

Fear buzzed in my head.

The therapist smiled, and I could see the pity in her eyes. She hadn't given us good odds. How much had Hank told her over the phone?

"I'm Marla. I'm glad you've chosen to come."

Hank let go of my hand. "Hank Sparks. This is my wife, Nacha."

My smile wasn't for Marla. Hank hadn't called me his wife in a long time.

"Hi. It's nice to meet you." Why had I said that? We were in counseling, not at a dinner party.

"Have a seat." She pointed at the small sitting area.

I headed straight for the love seat, but we'd look hopeless if Hank chose the armchair leaving me to flounder on my own.

After dropping onto one end of the love seat, I held my breath. Hank sat beside me, and I wanted to hug him.

"Nacha and Hank, I want you to feel like this is a safe place to share your feelings without feeling judged or ashamed. Some of the questions I ask may feel uncomfortable, but it's all a part of the healing process. Do you have any questions before we start?"

I shook my head. Didn't she realize that the judgement and shame came straight from my own brain? There was no safe place from that.

"Hank, how are things in the bedroom?"

So we're starting there. Okay. I stared at my hands, reminding myself that this was the best way to save my marriage—the counseling, not staring at my hands.

Hank inhaled, then let the breath escape at a painfully

slow rate. "The biggest problem, bedroom wise, is that hers is thirty minutes away."

"So you're separated?" Marla would probably be really good at poker.

He shrugged. "I guess that's what you'd call it."

Marla turned to face me. "Nacha, why don't you tell me why the two of you decided on marriage counseling."

"All right." I opened my mouth to start no less than five times, but words couldn't make it past the lump in my throat.

Hank shifted and angled toward me as he draped his arm across the back of the love seat. His thumb brushed along the back of my neck.

I glanced at him, and he nodded.

With him caressing my neck, I told her what happened, owning every bad decision. When I got to the part about admitting that we weren't divorced, Marla didn't completely cover her surprise. Maybe she shouldn't play poker.

Did I win something for shocking the therapist?

"That's why we're here." I squeezed the tissue in my hand, wondering when I'd grabbed it.

"Thank you for your honesty, Nacha." Marla leaned forward. "What are you hoping will happen by coming to counseling?"

I leaned into his hand. "I want us to live in the same house and be husband and wife again."

Marla cocked her head and focused on Hank. "In your eyes, what is the biggest problem in your marriage?"

His thumb stopped moving. "I don't trust her."

Marla asked how that made me feel, but I was too busy sobbing into my tiny tissue to answer her.

So far, counseling was going great. Just great.

～

Hank opened my car door. "I guess I'll see you next week."

"Yeah." Hopefully, I'd stop crying before then. I wiped my eyes. "If you think of any questions, call me. I'll answer." I stared at the keys in my hand.

"Nacha." Hank stepped closer.

I didn't want him thinking I was mad, so I met his gaze. "Yes?"

"It's hard for me too."

"I know."

He pulled me close and wrapped his arms around me. So much for not crying.

"I want this to work." He kissed the top of my head. "I really do."

Would it be weird to stand in a parking lot for a week? If I didn't move, maybe Hank would continue holding me.

"Me too." I slipped my arms around his waist. "Thank you for being supportive. I don't think I would've made it through the session otherwise."

He stepped back and brushed tears off my cheeks. "I should go."

"I'll see you later." I sat down behind the wheel, hoping I could make it out of Schatz county without Eli pulling me over. If that happened, I might never stop crying.

CHAPTER 21

*A*s luck would have it, Hank was working on Valentine's Day. I wasn't going to let that pass without making note of the day.

Covered in flour and powdered sugar, I added words to the last of the five-dozen heart-shaped cookies.

Cami took tiny bites of the one I'd let her have. "The icing is really yummy. I can't believe you made that many conversation hearts. Wouldn't it have just been easier to buy those little heart-shaped candies?"

"Maybe." But then I wouldn't have been able to have *Only You* on every single one.

Her gaze cut to the gift sitting on the chair. "You bought Hank an Xbox for Valentine's Day? That's an expensive hey-I'm-still-here-waiting-for-you gift."

"I got him one for Christmas. I'm just using the box." I chose not to address the other part of her comment.

Hank and I were on a path. It was long and winding, but we were moving forward. I hoped.

"While the icing dries, I'm going to run and change. Do

not eat any more of the cookies." I stopped in the doorway. "They tasted okay?"

"Delicious. You're a regular Paula Dean. How much butter is in these anyway?"

"You don't want to know." I laughed and hurried back to the bedroom. The unseasonably warm weather meant I could wear my sundress with the buttons down the front.

Hank loved that dress.

Driving like I had a wedding cake in my backseat, I made it to the station without ruining any of the cookies. Visions of the box hitting the floorboard kept me from speeding to see him.

I parked outside the station and texted Hank. *I'm here. I brought you Valentine goodies.*

I waited a minute then two without a response. The fire trucks were in the bays, but the ambulance was missing.

He was probably out on a call. Should I wait? Or leave?

As I was trying to decide, the ambulance pulled into the station.

Hank replied a minute later: *Just got back from a call. Give it to one of the guys.*

I didn't want to leave the cookies or the gift with anyone except Hank. *I don't mind waiting.*

My phone rang, and Hank's face filled the screen. "Hello."

"Hey." He sounded worn. "It'll be a bit. I need a shower, and I'm not good company."

"Take as long as you need. I'll be here." I meant that in every possible way.

He sighed. "Thanks."

To kill time, I scrolled through social media, then when that got boring, I played solitaire. I'd gotten good at solitaire in the last year.

Absorbed in my game, I nearly went through the windshield when Hank tapped on my window.

I tossed my phone aside and jumped out. "Hi."

Without a word, he pulled me into a hug and buried his face in my hair. I slipped my arms around his waist and rubbed his back. I didn't have to ask what was wrong. It was easy to guess. Not every call ended well for a paramedic. And even when they left the scene, the emotion followed them back to the station.

He pressed a kiss to my cheek, then stepped back and rolled his shoulders. "You brought goodies?"

"Cookies, and I brought you a gift. But you might not want to open it in front of the other guys." I handed him the box.

"Is that why you used thin paper and the console box?" He cracked a smile. "I won't make it two feet inside that door before they'll be pestering for me to open it."

"You can distract them with cookies." I pointed at the box buckled into the backseat. I wasn't taking any chances with those. They were a lot of work.

"You grab those and follow me in." He took a step, then stopped. "You didn't mention counseling to your mom?"

"I haven't told anyone. Not even about our phone calls. I guess I was just trying to protect us from everyone else's expectations. Who have you told?"

"No one. When I talked to your mom earlier today, she said she was worried about you because you turned down a cooking lesson on Tuesday but didn't say why. I think she was hinting for me to check on you."

"She keeps suggesting foods I should learn to cook to win you back."

"I'm not dragging this out because of that, but it is a nice perk." He started walking again. "Aunt Joji called and asked if you'd mentioned the tickets."

"Do they all think we talk often or are they trying to get us to talk?"

"I think it's the latter." He pushed open the door. "Guys, I'm not sure I can eat this many cookies. Anybody want one?"

He set the present down and lifted the lid on the cookie box. He picked one up. "Save me a few." To me, he said, "I'll walk you out."

Mitchell waved. "Thanks for the goodies, Hank's girl."

Hank looked back over his shoulder. "My wife's name is Nacha."

The room fell silent, and I fought the urge to laugh. "You're welcome. Save him a few, please." My heart did jumping jacks. When we stepped outside, I rubbed his arm. "Call if you want to talk."

"Thanks for coming by and for waiting."

"I wanted to see you. And I changed the reservations to August. I really don't want to go to Madrid without you."

He glanced back toward the door. "I should get back in there before they unwrap that gift without me there."

"It's just something to let you know I'm thinking about you." I hugged him. "All the time."

"Now I'm curious. Text me when you get home, okay?"

"I will, but I'm going to get some work done first."

"Do you like the new space?"

"Love it. There is even a tiny apartment in the back."

Hank chuckled. "Cami can always move in there."

"Just say when." I'd pack her stuff all by myself if need be.

"Bye." Hank strode away.

I drove down the street and around the corner to my new office. It was better suited to our needs, and I liked being close to Hank.

As I was walking toward the door, a deputy's car pulled up beside me. The window rolled down, and Eli smiled. "Evening, Nacha. It's kind of late to be working on a Friday, isn't it?"

One of the benefits of having our office in a small town was feeling like people looked out for each other. And Eli took his promise to protect and serve very seriously. It was kind of a shame he didn't seem interested in Cami.

I glanced at my keys to find the right one. "I spent the afternoon making cookies for Hank, so I'm here to play catch up."

He wrinkled his brow. "For Hank?"

"My husband. He's at work tonight at the fire station."

"I know who Hank is. I just thought . . . Never mind." He scratched his head and nodded toward the lingerie shop that had lights on in the back of the store. "Looks like you aren't the only one working late."

"You going in there to check on things?"

He shook his head a bit too emphatically. "Oh, no. No alarms. No complaints. Maybe there was a late shipment of . . . stuff."

Teasing Eli would be too easy and probably a lot of fun. But I resisted. "Night, Eli. I'll be here about an hour or so."

"Lock yourself in."

"I will."

I settled at my desk and opened the photos from my latest shoot. Going through the shots, I separated the keepers from the others. Then I worked on each photo. Focused on editing, I yelped when my phone beeped.

Hank's text made me laugh. *You warned me, but I didn't listen.*

Like the gift? I crossed my fingers as I waited for an answer.

Hank replied: *The guys thought the satin sheets and silk boxers were hilarious. Thanks for that. And silk boxers are one thing, but did you have to choose a pair with hearts on them?*

I laughed as I typed. *It was hearts or lips.*

I guess I should be thanking you. Was he standing outside while he texted?

I closed the laptop, ready to head home. *I bought a matching nightie.*

I saw that. And so did all the guys. Thanks for putting that in the box too. He followed his text with a winking emoji.

It seemed a shame to break up the set. And I know how you like visuals. I couldn't wait until I'd be able to model it for him.

You've already given me a great one. You headed home soon? His not so subtle change of subject was enough of a hint.

Packing up now. I'll text once I'm home.

He sent a single heart.

I tapped out another text: *One more thing: I can't wait to see those boxers.*

Hank replied: *You didn't see them when you bought them?*

I can't wait to see you wearing them. I hit send and waited for an answer.

The ever-so-meaningful thumb popped up.

While I completely regretted so many decisions, I'd learned a lot about myself and about my relationship with Hank. I loved him more now than the day he left.

It wasn't that I needed him or that he completed me. I wanted him. And I wanted to be there for him.

CHAPTER 22

For two months Hank and I attended weekly counseling sessions. He called more often in the evenings, and my hope grew.

But this week everything was different. Our next session was tomorrow night, and he hadn't talked to me since our last session a week ago.

Not panicking became more difficult. I added a little extra sugar to my coffee and grabbed a doughnut. Having a bakery right next door meant spending more time on my elliptical machine.

Haley walked in and closed the door as soon as I'd taken my first bite.

I wiped crumbs off my mouth. "What's up?"

She crossed her arms. "Any news?"

"No." This conversation wasn't helping me not worry.

"It's been months. I've met turtles that move faster than my brother." She dropped into a chair. "But Zach said that Hank definitely plans to be at the family getaway."

"I'm glad." I washed down the bitter taste rising in my throat with very sweet coffee, but it didn't help.

"Have you talked to him at all? The last couple of months, he's been distant even from Zach, but the two of them did go camping this past weekend."

"I've talked to him some. But he doesn't tell me much. I didn't even know they were going camping." I was glad Hank hadn't cut himself off from Zach. That friendship was important.

Haley bounced her leg. "And he's on some sort of spring-cleaning kick. I went by there, and the trashcans were full. That isn't like him. Anyway, I wondered if he'd said anything to you."

"He hasn't." I played connect the dots in my head.

Combined with Hank's sudden silence, the cleaning felt like bad news.

"I mentioned it to Zach, but he flashed me one of those tight-lipped smiles. The kind that doesn't really *tell* you anything." She pinched her lips. "I'm not really happy that my husband is keeping things from me. I even threatened to make him sleep on the couch." She coiled a strand of hair around her finger. "Not that I would actually do that—make him sleep on the couch. Since he knows that, he didn't spill the beans."

The panic she warned me not to have flooded my thoughts. Cleaning stuff out? The only time Hank had done a massive cleanout was when he'd moved out of his apartment when we got married. Was Hank planning to move? Had he gotten another chance at his dream job? Was that opportunity far away?

I tried to force a smile, but I couldn't make it happen. "A little bit of panic is in order, I think. But he would talk to you about moving out of the house, right? Y'all own it together."

"He hasn't said a word, *and* he put in that pool. I found out about it when a giant hole appeared in the backyard. When I think about that, I can't imagine that he's moving."

She paled. Shaking her head, she leaned forward. "Forget I said anything about moving. I'm sure he's not."

She didn't sound very sure.

I yanked out my phone and texted Hank: *Haven't heard from you all week. Miss you.* I stared at the phone, holding my breath.

His reply popped up a second later, and he used words instead of emojis. *I'll see you tomorrow night.*

Want to grab dinner after? I was putting myself out there even more than I already had.

Maybe. He wasn't giving me much information.

"Have you talked to anyone else about this?" I had dinner plans with Mama and Aunt Joji. If they knew about this, it would come up.

Haley shook her head. "I haven't. Zach keeps telling me not to worry. Maybe we should listen to him."

"Maybe." My head bobbed a yes, but my heart didn't agree. Something was going on, and it made me uneasy.

I thought of the look on Hank's face when I'd told him it was over. So much hurt. But the look when I admitted I'd never turned in the divorce papers was something else entirely.

Could Hank ever forgive me? Would he ever be able to trust me again?

Haley waved a hand in front of my face. "Did you hear me?"

"What?"

She pulled her hair into a scrunchie. "It'll be okay."

Would Hank talk to me before accepting the job? Wouldn't he have mentioned something in one of our sessions?

In the midst of the chaos in my brain, one thought grew bigger.

If he was moving, I wanted to go with him. It didn't matter where.

"Haley, if he is moving, I'm going to offer to go with him. He may shoot me down, but I need him to know that. And you need to know also."

She nodded, then started shaking her head. "No. That's not okay. I cannot run this business without you."

"I won't risk losing him. If being with Hank means living in some middle-of-nowhere town or even right on the beach, I'll go."

"In all the time I've known you, you've never even gone to the beach. I assumed you hated it."

"That's not what's important. Maybe I should text him and let him know."

She shrugged. "He hasn't answered any of my texts with words, he just sends a frustrating thumbs up."

I laughed. "Glad I'm not the only one that gets them."

"You got words. I'd consider that good news." She laid her hands flat on the desk. "You okay? I almost didn't tell you, but keeping it a secret didn't feel right."

"I'm glad you said something." Trying not to worry, I shot off another text. *Hank, I want to be with you even if it means leaving Texas.*

The maddening thumbs up appeared a second later. I turned the phone around so Haley could see. "And we're back to the thumb."

"I love my brother, but he can be frustrating." She checked her phone. "Want to come over tonight?"

"I have plans with Mama and Aunt Joji. You're welcome to join us. After that, I'm going to curl up and read."

"With Cami around? Good luck." Haley jumped up and walked to the door. "Have fun tonight. Zach and I are planning to—never mind. You don't want to know." She blushed.

I gave her a thumbs up.

"Not you too." Laughing, she groaned. "Y'all are totally meant for each other."

~

Two minutes late, I walked into the restaurant. Mama waved from a table in the corner.

"Have you had a good week? How many times have you gone out with Mateo?" I hadn't talked to her in several days but knew she'd probably seen Mateo. "I thought Aunt Joji was coming."

"She's here. And Mateo and I see each other often." She flashed a smile. "I like him. But we are taking it slow."

"I would never have guessed that you were sweet on him, Mama. *Never*." I hugged her before sitting down.

She swatted my arm. "He's very handsome."

"He is. I won't argue with you on that point. Did Aunt Joji say if she'd talked to Hank?"

Mama straightened her silverware, then crossed her arms. "She mentioned that he was going out of town."

Zach wasn't the only one with insider information.

Before I could grill Mama, Aunt Joji walked up. "Hello! Tomorrow—if you have time—I thought we'd go shopping. Oh, and you should pack that yellow dress you wore to Haley's wedding. It was quite flattering."

"I don't have the dress anymore. I left it on the patio at the resort when I rushed off. Since Hank didn't give it to me, I figured he didn't grab it."

"That's a shame. Where did you get it?"

"Hank bought it for me in a little shop in Colorado when we were on our honeymoon." I'd been so mad at him when I left Haley's wedding, losing the dress didn't seem like a big deal until much later. Wearing it that night was a huge mistake for multiple reasons.

"Do you remember the name brand? Maybe I could find it online and order one."

"There was no brand name. He bought it from a woman who'd made it by hand. That was the last one she had." I waited until the waiter was almost to the table, then said, "Besides, with Hank going out of town, who knows if he'll even make it to the getaway."

Aunt Joji and Mama exchanged a look. Was that panic? Yes, it was. And I felt justified in my worry.

Our waiter walked up to the table, waited until we looked at him, then smiled. "My name is Diego, and I'll be your server today. What can I get you to drink?"

"I'd like a cup of coffee and a glass of water."

"Lemon?" He wrote on his little notepad.

"Yes, please."

He took the other drink orders, then hurried away, leaving us to study the menus.

Aunt Joji opened hers but looked over the top at me. "He'll be there. I made him promise."

My hope that it would all be tied up in a pretty package was slipping. "Even if he doesn't show, we'll have a good time. Who will be there?"

"Your Mama is joining us. Mateo too. Of course, Haley and Zach, and Eli. He's a nice kid and he's practically family."

"He's not really a kid." I glanced at Mama who was staring at her menu like she couldn't understand the words.

Aunt Joji waved her hand. "You know what I mean. I like him. But it will only be a small group of us."

I tried to temper my excitement. "It sounds perfect. Maybe we should invite Cami. Would you mind?"

Aunt Joji beamed. "Yes, ask her. And let me know if I need to reserve another room. I'll reserve the whole place if I have to."

"Thank you so much for doing all of this." I watched

Mama continue to stare at the menu. "I'm glad Mateo is coming."

She didn't look up. "He's staying in his own room." Is that why she was being so quiet?

I bit back a laugh. "I didn't ask about that, but good to know."

Aunt Joji tapped the menu. "So many good choices." She laid the menu aside and rubbed her hands together. "I have some news."

"Did you meet some nice cowboy?" I met her gaze.

"Oh my, no. I'm not sure anyone could put up with me."

Mama laughed. "I think you mean *keep up* with you."

"That too." Aunt Joji danced her eyebrows. "I decided to settle here. I'm looking at buying a goat farm not far from Stadtburg."

"You what?" I stifled a laugh because it almost sounded like she wasn't joking.

"I'm going to buy a goat farm. Don't say anything. I'm going to announce it at our getaway."

As hard as I tried, I couldn't contain my laughter. "I cannot imagine you with goats."

"I signed up for a cheese-making class. And I might host tours or do petting zoo stuff. And maybe offer some of those goat yoga classes." She leaned in close and grinned. "I'll have to hire a few ranch hands. I wonder if I can talk them into doing yoga. People would pay to watch that I think."

I didn't even touch the idea of cowboys doing yoga. "Hank will want to interview all of them." I couldn't even imagine his reaction to this news.

Aunt Joji crossed her arms. "Hank will have to learn that he can't always have what he wants."

I didn't see that going well.

"I'm glad you aren't leaving town. It's been so fun having you here."

Her face lit up. "I've seen so much of the world, but here is the happiest I've been in a long time. "Now let's order food. I'm starved."

If Hank planned to leave town and asked me to go with him, at least Mama wouldn't be all alone. She had Aunt Joji and Mateo.

It would hurt to say goodbye, but the thought of being without Hank hurt much worse.

That evening, I pushed open the front door, and a strong odor flooded my olfactory senses. "Cami, what are you doing?"

She walked out of the kitchen, wearing an apron with *Kiss the Cook* plastered on the front. "Hey! You were gone a long time. I didn't have anything to do, so I ran to the store."

It was good that I'd asked about bringing her along for the family getaway. If this was what she did with an evening, I didn't even want to contemplate what she'd do with a weekend.

"Why does the house smell?"

"I'm making pickled squash. These would probably be better if we grew our own squash. Maybe we should plant some. Do you think April is too late to plant squash?"

"I think the vinegar smell is very strong. Let's open some windows."

"But it's humid outside."

"And it stinks in here." I opened a few windows.

When I walked back into the kitchen, Cami was slicing zucchini. "Have you seen Eli lately? Has he asked about me?"

"Y'all only met once."

"I guess that's a no." She sighed. "I'm not having any luck

meeting nice guys who don't look at me like I'm a three-year-old who has had too much candy."

"Give it time. You'll meet someone nice. It often happens when you least expect it. Hank's family is having a getaway weekend. Would you like to join us?" I pulled up the calendar on my phone and showed her which weekend.

She crinkled her nose. "Sounds fun, but things are a little tight. Daddy said he wasn't giving me any more money until I found a real job. But don't worry, I'll still pay you."

I pulled her into a hug. "I'm sorry you were cut off. Coming with me to the resort won't cost you a thing."

"Then I'm in. It sort of ruins my plans for the weekend, but whatever."

"Dare I ask?"

Cami grinned, and her eyes lit up. "I found some plaster stuff in your garage and was thinking about making a cast of my chest. It would be kind of artsy."

I envisioned her home alone and stuck in plaster. "What would you do if you couldn't get it off?"

Her grin widened. "Call the fire department."

"It's probably good that you aren't staying home. I'm not sure that's the best way to meet someone."

Cami stuffed zucchini slices into jars. "How did you meet Hank?"

The memory sparked a warmth in my chest. "Haley and I had just signed a lease on a small space. We bought furniture—the assembly required kind—and I learned that I'm not good at putting furniture together. Haley called her brother." I closed my eyes as I pictured him walking through the door that very first time. "I'd just picked up a box that was much too heavy for me when he pushed open the door. He took the box from me and said, 'You don't have to show off for me.' He showed up almost every day after that."

Cami pressed a hand to her chest. "Aww. I want that. So how did the magic happen?"

"He showed up one Friday evening. I was getting ready to go home but thought he was there for Haley. But he leaned against the doorframe of my office and crossed his arms. After hemming and hawing several minutes, he invited me to go out with him—dinner and dancing. I'd only known him a couple of months then, but I was smitten. Completely."

"How long did you date before he popped the question?"

"About six months."

Cami wrapped me in a hug. "I just know it's all going to work out."

"I hope so. I really hope so."

When she went back to her pickle-making, I ran out to the garage. I needed to hide the plaster.

CHAPTER 23

*S*howing up to counseling had gotten easier... until tonight. Five minutes past our start time, Hank still hadn't made an appearance.

I pushed back the cuticles on my nails. "I'm sorry. What was the question?"

Marla leaned forward. "You seem upset."

"This is the first time he's been late, and we haven't really spoken this week. I'm just... worried."

"Worried about what?" She always prodded me to say my frustrations out loud.

I glanced at the open door, then buried my face in my hands. "I'm worried that Hank has decided that he'll never trust me, and that he's given up on me."

"Do you trust him?"

I cradled the question, sitting with it a second before answering. "Completely. And I know he wouldn't move away without telling me, but what I did to him was horrible. At one point, I even told him it was over. I worry we can't recover from that."

The couch shifted, and either Marla was about to hug me, or Hank had walked in. I really didn't want Marla to hug me.

"Sorry I'm late." How much of that had Hank heard?

I sat up, and when I looked into his eyes, desire stared back at me. On impulse, I hugged him. "I missed you this week."

He patted my back as he pulled away. "Me too."

Marla got that look, like a preying cat who'd spotted a lone mouse. "Hank, what do you think of what Nacha said? Is recovery possible?"

"I wouldn't be here otherwise." His thumb brushed the back of my neck. "I made her a promise. I could never give up on her."

It didn't matter how the rest of this session went, I'd heard enough to fill my soul. If five years from now, we were still trying to figure it out, I'd—I'd be frustrated, but hopefully that wasn't how this would unfold.

At the end of the session, Marla pulled up her calendar. "Hank, I know you'll be gone next week, so we'll plan the session for the week after."

Why did everyone except me know that my husband was going to be out of town?

She scheduled our session, then clapped her hands. "And I'm giving you homework. Before we get together again, I want the two of you to spend time together . . . alone. But— and this part is important—I don't want you to focus on physical intimacy. I want you to be together without sex being the goal."

"We can do that." Hank stood and shoved his hands in his pockets.

I grabbed my purse. "Absolutely." Praying he didn't think that thirty minutes next to the pool during our getaway fulfilled the assignment, I followed him out.

We were silent until we arrived at my car. Asking about

dinner was a bad idea, so I smiled. "Call me about getting together."

He nodded. "You mentioned dinner. Does that still work?"

"Yes. I'd love that." My patience had been rewarded.

"Good. I made a reservation. Why don't I follow you to your house? You can ride with me to the restaurant."

My head bounced up and down much too vigorously. "Perfect."

I drove the short distance to the house, then walked to the truck.

He hopped out and opened my door. "I'm glad we're getting a chance to talk. There's something I need to tell you."

I grabbed his offered hand as I climbed up into the seat, loving how this felt like a date. Whatever it was he needed to tell me, I wasn't worried. I was too busy relishing the time with him.

He kept hold of my hand. "I meant what I said inside."

I kissed his cheek. "I know."

After a quick squeeze, he let go and ran back around to the driver's side.

When we walked into the restaurant, he didn't touch me or reach for my hand. But I was focusing on the positives.

Dinner conversation consisted of him talking about work and asking what else I was learning to cook.

It wasn't until the waiter set dessert on the table that Hank reached for my hand. "You probably heard that I was going out of town. I'm leaving tomorrow, and I'm not sure how long I'll be gone. No more than a week, I expect. I didn't want you to worry."

"So you'll be back for the mini reunion?"

"Aunt Joji threatened to invite Mitchell if I missed it. What I don't understand is why a family that sees each other almost every weekend needs a reunion. But what do I know?" He shrugged and chuckled.

"I'm guessing this is another of Aunt Joji's attempts to get us together."

"You think?" He trailed his thumb across my knuckles. "When I get back, we'll spend time together. I'll make dinner, and you can come over to the house."

"I'll get to see the new pool."

"Yeah. Bring your suit." His sarcasm was obvious.

That was exactly what I was going to do. I couldn't promise, I'd get into the pool, but I could wear a skimpy suit and hang out on the edge.

Wearing a swimsuit required a trip to the mall. I didn't own a bathing suit, let alone a skimpy one. I would remedy that while he was out of town.

~

When Hank walked me to the door that night, he didn't give me a kiss, but there was one in his eyes. I wanted to believe I wasn't imagining it.

CHAPTER 24

When Haley greeted me at the office door, I shook my head. "I know Hank left town. No, I don't know where he went or why."

"Dang it." She crossed her arms, then uncrossed them and propped her fists on her hips. "Being married to his best friend can be frustrating."

"Don't pester Zach. I'm glad Hank has someone to talk to." I carried my bag to my office.

Haley stayed right on my heels. "What about me? I'm his sister!" She dropped into a chair. "Zach drove him to the airport. They left about seven. So the flight is probably taking off about ten. I could search to see what flights are scheduled to leave about that time."

"Haley, don't worry about it. Hank will come back. And when he's ready to tell us where he went, he will."

Her eyes narrowed. "Spill it. You know something. Or did he say something to you?"

"He told me he was going out of town, that he didn't know how long he'd be gone, but that he'd be at the reunion." I inhaled. "Did I cover everything?"

"You seem so relaxed about it . . . like you *know* this trip is a good thing."

Putting an 'all good' label on the trip felt right, but I had no reason to believe the trip was good or bad. "I don't know that, but I trust him."

She tapped her chest, right over her heart. "I'll feel better when the two of you are back together." She sprang up out of the chair. "But I hate being the last to know things."

"Sorry." I glanced down at my phone when it beeped. I rarely had my sound off anymore. When my notifications sounded in public, people looked at me like I was twice my age. It was worth not missing a message or call from Hank.

He'd texted: *I really enjoyed dinner last night.*

It almost felt like old times. I read the message a second time before hitting send.

His reply made excitement dance in my chest. *Or like a new beginning.*

I sent a heart as my response. Messages like that offered more than a glimmer of hope that I'd be sharing that charming little cabin during the family getaway, which conveniently had a hot tub. Whatever skimpy swimsuit I bought could do double duty. All I had to do was convince myself to get in the water.

That involved a whole other level of trust.

When Cami's voice trailed down the hall, I jumped up to close my door.

"But when I went back out to the garage, I couldn't find the plaster, so no chesty wall art for above my desk."

Haley's giggle bubbled into a full-bodied laugh. "I'm pretty sure that wouldn't send the right impression about what type of photography we do."

"We could fix up that little apartment with a red sofa and plush rugs." Cami's ideas bordered on insane some days; other days, they were way over the line.

"No!" Haley tried to catch her breath. "I need to get some work done."

"I'm just teasing, you know. There's no way I'd smear plaster on me. Ick!"

I closed the door. My life had changed over the last few months into something that was almost perfect.

I knocked on my desk, which was probably only a good imitation of wood. Hopefully, that didn't matter too much.

Buried in work, I didn't come up for air until I left for a photo shoot. If the rest of the week stayed this busy, time would pass quickly.

I could hope.

That night, I tucked into bed, too tired to read. With the phone next to my pillow, I closed my eyes. Two seconds later, our song played, and I swiped at the screen. "Hello."

Hank waved. "I didn't mean to wake you. I guess it is kind of later there." He was in a different time zone, an earlier one.

"I don't mind. How was your flight?"

"Not too bad. I was hoping I'd be able to get my stuff done and hop a plane tomorrow, but it didn't work out that way. I'll be here a few days."

"I'm sorry for the delay." It took so much willpower not to ask where he was.

He set the phone down and walked out of view. "Thanks for not asking too many questions." When he reappeared, his shirt was absent.

I loved talking to him, but this was an extra-special treat.

"I trust you. Your sister, on the other hand, is being eaten alive by curiosity."

Hank laughed, which made me want to crawl through the screen and wrap my arms around him. "I'll have to get Zach something extra nice for Christmas for all that he's going through. Keeping secrets from my sister can be brutal."

I didn't like that phrase—keeping secrets.

In Hank's usual fashion, he responded to my thought. "It's temporary, Nacha. I'm not asking Zach to cover up a lie."

"Should I tell her that?"

"Won't matter. She signed up for it when she married my best friend. She told me to my face that she didn't want to interfere in the friendship."

"I know." Seeing Hank's passion on the topic reminded me of how hard it was for him to accept the idea of Zach and Haley as a couple.

The phone jostled, then Hank was in bed. "Tell me about your day."

For an hour, we talked like we did when we were first dating. I couldn't wait for him to get back to town.

We had a homework assignment to complete.

CHAPTER 25

*F*riday evening, I slipped the brand new, tiny, red bikini into my purse. All I had to do now was slip out of the house without telling Cami where I was headed.

My bags were packed for the family reunion, but the reunion wouldn't kick off until lunchtime. I didn't have time to think about how things would be with Hank at the resort.

Thinking of an excuse for tonight required creative thinking. I didn't really want to lie. Lies had caused me enough trouble.

But I wanted to spend time with Hank without people driving by the house and without people asking how it went.

"Hey, Cami. I'm—"

"Oh! There you are. Haley called me. They are starting the weekend festivities tonight. Your mom, her boyfriend, Aunt Joji, and I'm not sure who all else are headed over to their place. She wants us to come." She glanced down at my shoes. "Good, you're all ready to go."

"You go ahead. I have something else I need to do." Not a lie.

She shrugged. "Suit yourself." Two seconds later, she was in her car and backing out of the driveway.

When her taillights disappeared from view, an engine started across the street. Hank's truck pulled into the driveway. It was a good thing she didn't know what he drove.

I locked the door and ran out to meet him. "It's sweet of you to pick me up."

"More time together. That's the assignment, right?" He opened my door.

"Your timing was a bit too perfect. Would I be correct in thinking you suggested Zach host a backyard get-together tonight?"

He nuzzled my neck, which sent sparks—no pun intended—skittering up my spine. "I've always found your intelligence extremely attractive."

I hadn't signed anything agreeing to Marla's stipulations about the evening. Right now, I wanted one thing—to break Marla's silly rule.

I pressed closer. "Hank."

He touched a finger to my lips. "No kissing yet. It's way too early for that." With a wink, he helped me into the truck.

When did he become such a rule follower?

We were silent for the first few miles, but it didn't feel uncomfortable or awkward.

Hank broke the silence as we drove into Stadtburg. "I hope you don't mind that I haven't started cooking yet. Spending that time together seemed like a more appealing option."

"I'll even help."

"Sounds like a win." He pulled into his driveway. "And I had an ulterior motive for picking you up. If anyone happens to drive by, your car in the driveway would generate phone calls. Tonight, I'd rather not be interrupted."

"You want to focus on our homework."

"You read my mind." He held my hand as we walked to the door.

∽

"Want dessert now?" He picked up the plates.

I touched a finger to the bandage on his finger. "Did you hurt yourself?"

"It's fine."

"Why don't we sit out on the patio and talk? I still haven't seen the pool."

"Let me put these in the kitchen, then I'll show you."

Lingering by the back door, I dared to hope that all his comments about a new beginning meant that he'd made up his mind.

If he had, how long would he wait to tell me?

Hank pressed a hand to the small of my back as he opened the back door. "What do you think?"

What used to be an ordinary backyard was now landscaped with the pool and a hot tub as a focal point.

"Hank, it looks amazing. I didn't realize you were putting in a hot tub, too."

He pointed at a chair. "Sometimes, a hot tub is the perfect way to end a day."

"So I've heard." I sat down. "And you got a new grill."

"I did. I'm not thrilled with where it is. I think it's too close to the pool. I probably need to expand the patio. Be right back."

I waited while he ran inside. Maybe I'd suggest a soak in the hot tub. If I could be wrapped around Hank, I'd be able to handle being in the water.

He pulled a chair up next to me and handed over a cup. "Wine?"

"Please."

Water rippled, and the reflection from the porch light danced on the surface. Locusts and other creatures of the night were warming up their voices. My favorite wine rolled over my taste buds.

Hank brushed his hand on mine before lacing our fingers together. "Thank you for agreeing to counseling. Forgiving you was a long process, but knowing you were committed to getting back together helped."

"I love you, Hank. I wish I could go back in time and change so many things."

A sadness settled in his eyes. "Like what you said before leaving the wedding?"

"I was mad and embarrassed. I should never have said those words."

"Did you mean it?"

I took another sip of wine, aching from the memory. "I sobbed all the way home. I was mad and embarrassed, but the tears were because of regret. When Eli pulled me over that night, I was a mess."

"He what?" Hank furrowed his brow.

"My foot rested a bit too heavy on the accelerator. Poor guy was really flustered. I figured word had gotten around."

"I didn't know." He balanced his cup on the arm of his chair. "Those words are hard for me to forget. I think—"

The wind gusted and blew his cup, splashing his drink all over him. He jumped up, then reached under the grill to pick up the cup. On his way back up, his head connected with the edge of the BBQ pit. With his eyes squeezed closed, he grabbed his head, mumbling words he never said in front of children. He stepped backward, tripped over a potted plant, and splashed into the pool.

How hard had he hit his head? Without stopping to think, I launched into the pool feet first. Why did he have to fall into the deep end?

When I felt his shirt, I shoved on him, hoping I could get him to the shallow end. Gagging and choking, I pawed at the water, determined not to cling to Hank. Climbing on him would pull him under. Sinking, I tried not to breathe in water and failed. A lot. When my feet touched bottom, I kicked upward. Sputtering, I shoved on Hank when he grabbed me.

Finally opening my eyes to see why he wasn't floating, I met Hank's gaze.

"What are you doing?" He hugged me close, keeping my head out of the water.

"Saving you." I laughed at how stupid it sounded.

"Considering that you can't swim, after I rescue you from the pool—again—maybe you can explain that to me."

I looped my arms around his neck. "I didn't know how hard you'd hit your head. If you fell in unconscious—"

"I was cursing, Nacha. Perfectly conscious." He swam to the shallow end, keeping my face safely out of the water.

"I panicked."

He sat on the step and pulled me into his lap. "Don't ever jump in the pool again."

"Until I learn to swim." I pulled back far enough to look him in the eye.

He blinked. "You what?"

"Will you teach me? I don't mean tonight."

"You get yourself a skimpy little swimsuit, and I'll give you private lessons." He danced his eyebrows.

I poked his chest, then dropped a kiss on his neck. "But I'm serious about learning."

"I'll teach you. That would make me feel better. As often as you end up in the pool." He laughed.

His hand slipped behind my neck, and he pulled me to his lips. Desire and hope exploded as our mouths communicated without words. He let loose a soft moan, and I pressed in closer.

His hands moved down to my hips, and after pulling away, he snagged one more kiss. "Stay with me tonight."

I sealed my lips to his, too happy for words.

He brushed my cheek as he pulled away.

Leaning into his hand, I laughed. "I don't care about Marla's suggestion."

Instead of laughing, he furrowed his brow. "Let's get you out of the pool. Then we'll talk."

I scrambled out of the water and crossed my arms. "Talk about what?" Refusing to cry, I blinked and wiped pool water out of my eyes. That was all it was—pool water.

He guided me to a chair, then sat beside me. "What I started to say before you decided to go for a swim—" He dragged his arm across his face. "This isn't the way I planned this. Come with me."

"We'll drip all over the floor." I preferred the darkness. It hid my disappointment.

Hank grabbed both of my hands. "Please."

I followed him inside, down the hall, and into the bedroom.

"Close your eyes."

Being in the bedroom with my eyes closed was more in line with where I thought the evening was going before he dropped the we-need-to-talk line.

With my hands covering my face, I waited.

"Okay, you can open them now."

I dropped my hands only a second, then covered my mouth.

Hank was on one knee. "Ignacia Sparks, will you marry me *again*?"

I nodded, but words tumbled out of my mouth. "We're still married."

Reaching into his pocket, he swallowed. "You said it was over, so I'm going to need you to say the words *again* in front of a minister."

What he'd said outside now made sense.

I hugged him. "I do. I will. What will we tell him?"

"We'll tell him we're *tightening* the knot." Hank held out my engagement ring. "Cami isn't so bad. She helped me sneak around to get what I needed." He slipped the ring on my finger, then tore the bandage off his.

I didn't have room in my head to think about Cami right now.

A tattoo circled his ring finger. "Forever, Nacha. I can't take it off. It never goes away. I love you."

I dropped to my knees and kissed him. "When?"

"When did I get the tattoo? While I was out of town."

Poking at his chest, I laughed. "I meant, when are we going to get married again?"

He brushed a finger along my cheek. "I planned to ask you tomorrow when we were all at the resort. Since I had a pretty good idea of what you'd say, I also called a minister. Your brothers and their families will be there too."

I threw my arms around him. "Yes, I want this. I want you."

CHAPTER 26

*H*ank handed me a towel, then dropped another on the puddle created while we'd made up for lost time. "Help yourself to whatever you want to wear. We can run your stuff through the washer and dryer."

I grabbed his hand. "I was thinking—"

He wagged his finger. "No silk boxer viewing until after you say I do."

"Hank!"

"Abstinence makes the heart grow fonder."

I'd missed his corny jokes and amazing sense of humor. "That's not even the right saying."

"If the swimsuit fits." He grinned.

"Since we are only going to be talking, I thought maybe we could do it in the hot tub."

His gaze swept downward. "But you . . . don't have a . . ." It wasn't hard to guess what he was thinking. "Sure. We can do that. I just won't turn on the back-porch lights. The water isn't deep. You'd have to work pretty hard to get completely under water."

"And you'll hang on to me."

He dipped his head and whispered in my ear. "I'll keep my hands wherever you want."

"Let me grab my purse. My swimsuit is in it." With the towel wrapped around my wet dress, I hurried down the hall, then returned to the bedroom carrying my very small purse.

His smile widened. "If your swimsuit fits in there, I can't wait to see it." He walked toward his dresser.

"I'll change in the—" I headed toward the door.

"No. Stay in here." He swung his swimsuit in a circle and blew me a kiss as he walked out of the room.

When I'd shopped for the swimsuit, I'd been thinking of Hank. With very little fabric and lots of strings, the suit didn't cover much. I peeled off my dress, wiped up the floor, and tied on my bikini. Standing in front of the mirror, I imagined his excitement. The red fabric popped against my olive skin.

He'd love it.

Whistling, he knocked on the door. "You decent?"

"Not hardly, but you can come in."

The door opened, and Hank dropped the clothes he'd carried in. The next thing I knew, we were tangled together on the unmade bed, kissing like we'd just discovered love.

When we finally stopped to catch our breath, he grinned. "Oh, I've missed you. And all joking aside, while it's taking every last bit of willpower not to pull on these strings,"—he touched my hip—"tonight was supposed to be about talking, and if I pull on this, I won't be talking."

I kissed his cheek. "Tonight can be for conversation and cuddling." If this was my penance for the ways that I'd hurt him, I could handle it . . . for one night.

"Tomorrow will be for nuptials and nakedness. How's that for alliteration?" His laughter echoed off the walls. "Are you sure about getting in the hot tub because—you know—you hate water."

"I'm sure. But I'll probably cut off circulation in your hand because I'm gripping it too tight when I step in."

He sat up. "I won't let you go."

I eased up behind him. "You spent most of last year working out, didn't you?"

"Had to take out my frustration somewhere."

I climbed onto his back. "You look amazing."

"If I didn't make that completely obvious minutes ago, you do too. But you haven't changed." He carried me piggyback outside, then put me down next to the hot tub. "Want me to go in first so you can see how deep it is?"

"That's a good idea." I was determined to get into the water without panicking.

He stepped in, and I relaxed a little. His chest was still mostly visible.

"There are seats on the sides. Just hold my hand as you step in. I won't let go."

I nodded but didn't step into the water.

"You don't have to do this, Nacha."

"I want to." I dipped my toes in the water, and warmth tingled on my skin. "It feels good."

"Whenever you're ready." He held out his hand.

Slipping my fingers into his hand, I breathed in deep. I could do this.

I took the first step, squeezing his hand. The second step was a bit easier. When my feet touched the bottom, I hugged Hank. "I think I'll just stay wrapped around you like this."

"I have no complaints." Chuckling, he guided me to the side and pulled me into his lap as he sat down. With his arms around me, he rested his chin on my shoulder. "We've covered many topics in our sessions, but there is one thing I haven't told you."

"Okay?" I trusted him, but his tone made me curious.

"The person who suggested that maybe there was too

much distrust and hurt was a woman like you suggested that day outside the fire station. Tandy was the one who said it. She's probably pushing seventy. But don't tell her I said that because I'm not great at guessing women's ages, and if she's only fifty, she'll hate me."

Laughing, I drew hearts in the water droplets on his chest. My amusement only fueled him.

"I've had to go to her house to get the same bowl off the same shelf nearly every week. I'm not sure how the bowl gets back up onto the very high shelf, but I think I'm being played. So, when you move in, if the silver-haired lady next door gives you dirty looks, you'll know why."

I never would have imagined being so content in the water. But with his embrace and the warmth of the hot tub, everything felt perfect. "She sounds like a hoot."

"She's a something." He pressed a kiss to my cheek.

"Is she the one who writes romance novels?"

"Yep. She has books with bare-chested men on the covers spread out on her coffee table. I think she just likes looking at them."

"Hank."

He continued his trail of kisses down to my neck. "Hmmm?"

"When you go help her with the bowl, please wear a shirt."

"Always." He trailed his fingers along my back, stopping occasionally to toy with the strings. "I'm not sure where I put the deck of cards."

"I have no interest in playing War tonight." I arched my back as his hands trailed lower. "If you find another job opening, you should apply. I'll go with you, wherever that is."

"We'll see. I like living here. It's near your mom and Haley. Aunt Joji is even going to be living here now that she bought that goat farm. Our life is here."

"But your dreams." I didn't want to be the reason he settled for something less than what he wanted. "And how do you know about the goat farm?"

He crinkled his brow. "Oops. I wasn't supposed to say anything. But you already knew."

"I did. I have a feeling that when she announces it, it won't be a surprise to anyone. And I want you to follow your dream, Hank."

"The dream of seeing a baby in your arms and then growing old with you is much more important to me than being a medic in a helicopter."

I sealed my lips to his, overwhelmed by what he'd said. "Mama wants a granddaughter."

"I'll do my best." His lips brushed my shoulder. "But not until tomorrow."

I leaned my head on his chest. "I had no idea a hot tub could be so relaxing."

"When you aren't trying to breathe it in, the water can be nice."

Ticking through what I'd need for tomorrow, I pushed away from him, ready to get out. "I'm not changing my mind about tomorrow, but I have no idea what to wear." I leaned toward the edge of the hot tub.

Hank grabbed me around the waist. "I have something for you inside."

"Something for me to wear?"

He nodded. "I got so distracted by your leap into the pool and by that swimsuit, I forgot to give it to you. Do you want to go in now?"

"No. Let's stay here longer." I snuggled back into his lap.

"It'll be a little sad to leave this house now that this amazing pool is here, but I'm sorta set on living *with* you. And not Cami . . . in case that needs to be said."

"Poor Cami. I'm not sure what she's going to do. But if

you're okay with it, I'd like to sell our house. You work in Stadtburg, and now I do too. Let's live here. Haley won't care, will she?"

"Haley will be thrilled, but are you sure? The kitchen isn't as big."

"You can build an outdoor kitchen near the pool."

That was a win for me because he'd cook more.

We spent a half hour tangled in each other's arms, kissing and talking.

"Once I'd decided that I didn't want to live without you, I went radio silent. I spent the week cleaning stuff out, getting ready to move back home. Also, I knew I couldn't talk to you and not say something. I almost blew it in counseling. I wanted you to know, but I wanted to surprise you."

"I loved hearing that you'd never give up on me. I think I needed to hear that."

"Let's go inside." He scooped me into his arms and carried me to his bedroom. "Let's get into some dry clothes, then you can open your gift."

"I didn't pack a change of clothes in my purse." I shrugged.

He handed me a t-shirt. "This is the best I can offer you." Grinning, he tugged on the strings on the back of my top. "Want my help taking this off?"

"I do."

Chuckling, he stepped away and dug clean clothes out of his drawer. "You keep practicing those two words."

When we were both somewhat dressed and sitting on the bed, Hank handed me a perfectly wrapped present. "Open this."

I peeled off the tape before taking the paper off in one large piece.

He rolled his eyes. "You must've been a blast at Christmas as a kid." Wearing only a pair of gym shorts, he flopped back onto the pillows. "We've been talking all evening, and you haven't asked me where I went."

"I figured you'd tell me." I lifted the lid off the box. My yellow dress lay in the box. "You saved my dress."

"No. It couldn't be saved. It turns out that Coke and chlorine are very bad for that type of fabric. As I was told *multiple* times."

"But . . ." I pulled the dress out and held it up in front of me. "I don't understand."

"I flew to Colorado and begged the nice shop lady to make me another one. She wanted to know why. After telling her our story, she made a new dress in three days. Just for you. I paid her of course."

"Hank, that is—you are the most romantic man ever."

"Go hang your dress, then come back over here."

After slipping the dress on a hanger, I snuggled up next to Hank and rested my head on his chest. "I love you."

Grinning, he gave me a thumbs up.

Whether or not we followed the advice of our marriage counselor was nobody's business.

CHAPTER 27

Waking up with Hank spooned behind me and his arm draped over me made it hard—pretty much impossible—to get out of bed. If we didn't have big plans for the day, I'd stay right here beside him.

While he slept, I thought through what I'd need. I had the dress, but shoes? Aunt Joji had replaced my broken pair, but they were at my house. I glanced at the clock on the nightstand. If I left now, I could be back in just a little over an hour. It wasn't that late. What time had Hank arranged for the minister to arrive?

I lifted Hank's arm and inched toward the far side of the bed.

He pulled me back toward him. "Don't get up. We have time."

"I need to run home and get—"

"Your shoes are in the closet. Please lie down."

"How did you know Aunt Joji bought me new ones."

"I didn't. I found them in your closet."

I snuggled back into his arms. "Then I will stay here if that makes you happy."

"I've missed this, and I've missed you." He pressed a kiss to my shoulder.

"What time is everything happening?" I trailed my finger up and down his arm.

"Ceremony at eleven. Lunch planned at noon."

As much as I loved him cuddled up behind me, I wanted to see his face. I rolled over, and we were nose to nose. "And after that?"

"Don't make plans." The heat and desire in his gaze warmed my whole body.

Bouquets were created so brides would have something to do with their hands. But I didn't have one, and therefore, had no idea what to do with my hands. I waited just outside the small garden area as family and friends took their seats. Having my family and our closest friends here to watch us renew our vows was perfect.

Mama whispered with Mateo, and I wondered if we'd be celebrating another marriage soon.

Cami's hands waved as she chatted with Eli, but he wasn't doing any talking. She might be a little too much for that poor guy.

When I heard footsteps, I turned toward the path. Hank and the minister walked toward me. For some reason, I'd expected someone younger. But this guy had grey near his temples and very kind eyes. There was warmth in his smile.

My sweet husband had planned every last detail. Letting someone else do the planning wasn't what I was good at. But he'd done such a great job. Today was so perfect, I felt spoiled.

With his hand behind his back, Hank smiled. "Someone once told me that ladies like flowers, so these are for you." He handed me a small bouquet of red Gerber daisies. "Reverend Miller, this is my wife Nacha."

The minister extended his hand. "Everyone calls me Mad Dog."

Snickering, I bit my lip. "And I thought today couldn't get any better. I'm guessing Hank explained our situation."

Nodding slowly, Mad Dog slipped a Bible out of his pocket. "He did, and I feel privileged to be here to help you renew your vows. Would you like to be called Ignacia or Nacha?"

"Nacha. Thank you so much." I clasped Hank's hand. "I think everyone is here and ready."

Mad Dog Miller, my new favorite minister, grinned. "I'll let y'all have a minute. But only a minute. Don't go sneaking off to your room." He winked. "I'll be up front."

Hank pulled me close. "One of the best things about today is I'm not nervous, only excited."

"I know." I touched his face, wishing I had both hands free. "I'd promised myself I'd never say those two words again."

He pinched his lips together, controlling his emotions. Then twinkles danced in his eyes. "If you want to see the boxers..."

I kissed him. "Don't make me wait. Go up to the front."

"Love you." He brushed my cheek, then stepped away.

I waited until everyone was positioned in front. He hadn't mentioned music, so I counted to five before stepping to the end of the small aisle.

The wedding march started to play, and Cami giggled as she held up her phone. "Now you can go. But slowly."

With my gaze fixed on Hank, I walked to the front, probably not as slowly as Cami had planned. Haley grinned and took the bouquet.

Hank clasped my hands.

Mad Dog cleared his throat, getting everyone's attention. "Friends and family, we are gathered here today to celebrate the marriage of Hank and Nacha. If anyone has an objection to these two sharing their lives, forever hold your peace. That ship has sailed."

Laughter erupted, which only made the day better.

Hank winked, and my every nerve ending tingled with anticipation of being alone with him.

The ceremony continued with laughter and tears. Most of the tears were mine. But even Hank wiped away one or two.

When we got to the iconic part, the part I thought I'd never say again, Hank lifted an eyebrow.

Mad Dog smiled at me. "Do you, Nacha, take Hank as your lawfully wedded husband? Do you promise to love, honor, cherish, respect, and comfort him, in good times and bad, in sickness and in health? To share your joys and sorrows, help him when he needs help and turn to him first when you need help, and forsaking all others, to be faithful to him alone?"

Meeting Hank's gaze, I squeezed his hands. "I do."

Without waiting for the right time, he leaned in and kissed me.

The reverend chuckled. "Usually we do the rings next."

"Sorry." Hank grinned.

We exchanged rings. And I loved that under his wedding band was another ring that would always be with him.

It had taken me a year of being unhappy to appreciate my happily ever after.

After Mad Dog announced us to the crowd, Hank and I hurried back down the aisle and found a quiet, out-of-the-way spot while the rest of our family and friends went inside for lunch.

He dropped kisses on my neck. "I'm not hungry."

"Neither am I, but we should at least make an appearance. A short one."

He trailed a finger down the zipper on the back of my dress. "Emphasis on the word short."

I grabbed his hand and pulled him toward the building.

When we stepped inside, everyone exploded in a cheer.

Most of my favorite people were in this room, and I'd never felt more at home.

Aunt Joji handed Mad Dog a plate, insisting he go through the buffet line first.

Hank kissed my cheek. "I'm going to go thank the minister."

"Please tell him how perfect it was."

Cami ran up. "I hope you don't mind that I let your hottie rummage through your room."

"Not a bit. Thank you for helping him surprise me."

She stepped closer. "Speaking of hotties, that reverend—oh my!"

"He said to call him Mad Dog. And don't you think he's a tad old for you?"

Fanning herself, she glanced over her shoulder. "I'm just going to sit by him. There's no harm in gawking."

"What about Eli?"

She shook her head. "He's adorable, but he looks at me like he doesn't know what to do with me."

"I think he's a bit shy."

"Shy isn't really my type." She laughed, then chewed her bottom lip. "I just wanted you to know that it means a ton that you included me today."

I wrapped her in a hug. She'd become almost a little sister. "It wouldn't have been the same without you. I'm glad we've become friends."

"And I'll find someplace else to live. Living with newlyweds would be weird. No, thank you."

"I'm moving in with Hank. We'll be selling the house, but you can stay there until someone buys it."

She hugged me again. "Thank you."

"Go enjoy the food."

She strolled across the room and took a seat next to Mad Dog. Cami really needed to meet someone well-matched to her energy level. Despite Harper's insistence that Haley and I avoid setting him up, I wanted him to meet Cami. Figuring out how to make that happen would have to wait for another day.

I made my way around the room, hugging people and thanking them for being in on my surprise. Then I joined Hank near the door. "I'm ready."

He waved to our guests. "Enjoy lunch." He scooped me up as everyone laughed. "It's kind of a treat getting to carry you when you aren't drenched from taking a dip in the pool."

He carried me out of the building and down the pebbled path.

With my arms around his neck, I brushed my lips on his ear. "Are you wearing the boxers right now?"

"Want me to model them for you?" He pushed open the door to the cabin and carried me to the bed.

I wanted that and so much more. Reaching for his buttons, I trailed kisses along his jaw. "I do."

EPILOGUE

HARPER

Being invited to Hank and Nacha's pool party had me on high alert. Nacha didn't seem the type to set people up, but she was in business with Haley. Hopefully, I wasn't about to attend my own blind date. Because the only thing worse than actually going on a blind date was being set up in front of an audience.

I was done with blind dates. Dating in general wasn't going all that well. I'd even met someone cute, but she ran off before I could get her name. That mystery blonde had taken up residence in my thoughts, and just maybe she'd made a brief appearance in a dream or two. Sadly, I'd probably never see her again.

Returning my thoughts to the party, I glanced at the few cars parked on the street. It wasn't like I didn't know Hank and Nacha at all. I did have a hand in getting him his dream job. Maybe that was why I'd been invited. I crossed my fingers and walked to the door.

Hank yanked it open before I knocked. "Hey there. Come on in. Everyone else is out back."

"I wasn't sure what to bring. Because believe me, you

don't want anything I cooked or baked." I held up two jugs of sweet tea. "So I brought this."

"Perfect! Cami was just asking if we had any. I'm sure when you get out there, Nacha and Haley will introduce you." Hank chuckled.

"Dang it. I was hoping the invitation was just an invitation." I followed him to the back door.

"Thanks to you, I'm working my dream job and living here in Stadtburg. I didn't think that was possible." He patted my shoulder. "You're my friend, Harper. You'll always be welcome at our house."

"Thanks." I inhaled as he reached for the door handle. "I think I'm ready. Is she at least cute?"

"I'm not saying a word." Hank was not making this easy.

I stepped onto the porch and nearly dropped both gallons of tea. My mystery blonde sat on the side of the pool, splashing water with her feet.

Lady luck was smiling on me.

I nudged Hank without tearing my gaze from my dream come to life. "Is that Cami?"

"The one and only. If she likes you, you'll know it."

Before any of the ladies noticed me, I slipped back inside. "I'll leave this tea in here." I found the red plastic cups and filled two with tea before sticking the jugs in the fridge.

I walked back out and headed right toward Cami. "Did someone order a sweet tea?"

She glanced over her shoulder, and her entire face lit up. Scrambling to her feet, she giggled.

This was the type of hello I'd dreamed about.

"My superhero!" Before I could respond, she threw her arms around my neck, sending both cups flying.

That mess could be cleaned up later. I'd just found my mystery woman and she'd called me her superhero. This was the best party ever.

I picked her up and spun her around. "It's good to see you too. You look a bit different today." After a quick, polite glance at her swimsuit, my gaze snapped back to her face. I'd say that was her best feature, but she was like a window display—every inch was perfect.

She pressed a finger to my lips. "We are not talking about what I was wearing last time. Never ever."

Nacha slipped her arms around Hank's waist. "Be careful saying never. Life doesn't always work that way."

"Thankfully." Hank kissed the top of her head. "Everyone swim. That's why I had them put in the pool. We go to Zach's for Cornhole and my house for the swimming hole."

Nacha looked up at him. "Your house?"

"*Our* house." He scooped her up. "Think we should get in?"

She nodded and gripped his neck. "But just in the shallow end."

Cami spun to face the pool but tilted her head back and whispered to me. "Nacha has issues with water."

"Then why is she getting in the pool?"

"Hank." Cami turned back to face me. "I just cannot believe you are here. This is like the best day ever."

"I'm really glad you think so."

Nacha clung to Hank's back as he walked around the shallow end.

One by one, the other party goers climbed or jumped into the pool.

I unbuttoned my shirt. "Go ahead and get in. I'll join you as soon as I clean up the cups."

Cami stared at my chest. "I think I'll just watch you work."

Haley splashed water at Cami. "Are you just going to stand there staring at the poor man?"

Cami grinned and pointed at me as she looked over her shoulder. "He's a total hottie."

Haley shook her head. "I think as a fireman, he probably hears that a lot."

"You're a fireman?" Cami sighed, her eyes twinkling with—was that admiration?

"In the flesh."

She patted my chest. "Most definitely."

I threw the cups in the trash, and she splashed water on the area where the tea landed. "It was my fault they fell, and I don't want the patio to get sticky."

"Good idea."

With her head cocked, she eyed me. "If I accidentally swallow water in the pool, will you rescue me?"

There wasn't a shy bone in her body, which made her amazing in my book.

"Absolutely."

"How long would I need to hold my breath before you gave me mouth-to-mouth?" She grabbed my hand and tugged me toward the pool, then stopped. "I'm kidding. Sort of. You know what! I don't even know your name."

"Ethan Harper. But everyone calls me Harper."

She giggled. "Harper the hero."

My dating life had definitely taken a turn for the better.

∼

Keep reading for a BONUS epilogue.

BONUS EPILOGUE

HANK

As much as I adored spending time in the pool with Nacha, I wasn't looking forward to this afternoon. I liked being married to and sharing a bed with Nacha—and all that went with that. Teaching her to swim could have ill effects on our relationship.

But she'd insisted. Tomorrow, we embarked on our trip to Madrid, and she wanted to learn at least a little before we left.

I'd never taught anyone to swim, so I'd been watching videos, getting ideas for what to teach.

As it was now, when we were in the water, she clung to me. I didn't mind that a bit . . . especially when she wore that teeny red bikini.

I splashed water on my face, trying to get my thoughts back on track.

She stepped out onto the patio. Instead of wearing a coverup, she wore my shirt. Slowly my clothes were moving to her side of the closet, but I didn't care.

Without shorts on, Nacha had legs a mile long. And I drank in every inch.

I crossed my arms on the edge of the pool and rested my chin on them. She had a whole routine. After stepping outside, she'd lay the towels in the sun, kick off her shoes, and then take off that t-shirt.

I loved watching.

And she knew it.

Instead of yanking it off, she'd tease a little.

Today, she went through the same routine. She turned, giving me her back, then glanced back over her shoulder. Clutching the hem, she lifted slowly.

The shirt hadn't made it up very far, and I knew pool time would be all about swimming. She was wearing what I liked to call her company suit—the one piece that covered lots of skin. She always wore that one when we had company. I preferred the red bikini, but when she wore that one, we never actually got around to lessons.

She tossed the shirt aside and strolled to the edge of the pool. "Hi."

"Before you climb in, I just want to remind you that you promised to love me for better or for worse."

She rolled her eyes. "I've been in the pool with you, Hank."

"But you've never been in the pool without hanging onto me for dear life. To swim, you will have to let go of me."

"I know." She stepped into the water after taking a deep breath. "And I know I will have to put my face in the water."

"That's where we'll start." I moved closer and stretched out my hand.

Lips pinched together, she gripped my fingers. Her fear was obvious, but so was her courage.

I pulled her close. "I think that's the first time you've stepped into this pool without turning my hand white in the process. You've made progress."

"I'm really trying."

"I'll never be far away."

She nodded.

"Pull in a deep breath, as deep as you can. Then put your face in the water." I squeezed her hand. "You don't have to let go of my hand right now. We'll work up to that."

After filling her lungs, she bobbed her face into the water. Sucking in air before she was completely out of the water, she choked.

"You okay?" I hadn't realized how hard it would be to watch her do this.

Squeezing my hand, she inhaled again, then put her face in the water.

I held onto her hand. "One. Two. Three."

Grinning, she popped up and wiped her face. "That wasn't so bad."

"Can you do it again and keep your face in the water until I count to five?"

"I think so." She glanced at her hand in mine. "You've got me?"

"Always."

With her face fully under the water, I counted to five.

Her smile was even brighter. "What's next?"

"Let's do that one more time, then you can try it without holding my hand."

She made it look easy.

When she came up out of the water, I kissed her. "Great job."

"I wouldn't trust anyone else to teach me." She trailed a finger down my chest. "Let's do a little more."

"Since you asked nicely. This is what I'm going to have you do next." I stretched out and floated on my belly. "I'll hold your hand the first time."

She licked her lips, determination in her dark eyes. "I think I can do it without holding your hand. Five count?"

"If you can."

With her arms spread wide, she floated while I counted, then got back on her feet. "Now I know what to do if I ever fall in the water."

"I'll also teach you to float on your back. But before we do that, I want you to swim a little. You'll just kick your feet, and that will move you through the water." I demonstrated.

Twenty minutes later, she was crossing the shallow end on her own. "I did it!"

"You aren't quite ready for the Olympics, but you're getting there."

Tears glistened in her eyes. "You're a great teacher."

I pulled her up against me. "I think that's enough lessons for today."

"Hank, I know it's not easy teaching me. But thank you. It's important to me to be able to get into the pool without you in case there was an emergency or anything . . . especially now." She spun, pressed her back to me, and pulled my hand to her stomach. "You'll have to read about how to teach little ones to swim. And we should consider fencing off the pool."

Fireworks exploded inside my head. "Are you telling me . . . ?"

Leaning against me, she nodded. "I am. I'm not far along, so I'd rather not say anything to others right now."

"We're going to have a baby." I laughed and kissed her cheek. "Well, *you* are going to do all the work at this stage. I just—wow! A baby."

She turned and circled her arms around my neck. "Thank you for forgiving me but mostly for loving me and for letting me love you."

Instead of trying to explain how much she meant to me, I pulled her to my lips. Some truths my mouth couldn't convey with words. Kisses, however, offered an entirely different vocabulary.

~

Want to read Cami and Harper's story?
Visit RemiCarrington.com for information about *One Choice I'd Never Make*!

A NOTE TO READERS

Thank you for reading! I hope you loved Hank and Nacha's story. Finding the right balance of hard work and forgiveness challenged me. Falling in love might be easy. Staying love often takes work.

As for the food mentioned, I highly recommend *carne guisada* (beef simmered with tomatoes and bell peppers, onion, garlic, and Mexican seasonings), *polvorones* (similar to pink sugar cookies), and *buñuelos* (flaky sweets sprinkled with cinnamon sugar). My grandpa made the best *carne guisada* I've ever tasted. But when it came to tamales, my grandma holds that title.

She and her sisters used to make them on Christmas Eve. My mom learned to make them, and then I learned. I still make them almost every year. It's a lot of work, but soooo worth it.

I'm so excited for Cami and Harper's story. They are both fun character who need to fall in love. And if you want to read about Nacha's mama and her relationship with Mateo, grab a copy of the story, *Christmas Surprise*.

Be sure to check out my website.
www.RemiCarrington.com
It has information about upcoming releases and my other sweet romances.

ALSO BY REMI CARRINGTON

Never Say Never

Three Things I'd Never Do

One Guy I'd Never Date

Two Words I'd Never Say Again

One Choice I'd Never Make

Three Rules I'd Never Break

Two Risks I'd Never Take Again

One Whopper of a Love Story

Stargazer Springs Ranch

Love happens at Stargazer Springs Ranch. Fall in love with cowboys and spunky women.

Cowboys of Stargazer Springs

Love is spreading on Stargazer Springs Ranch. The ranch hands are falling in love.

Bluebonnets & Billionaires series

Swoon-worthy heroes with lots of money (and even more heart) will have you sighing, laughing, and falling in love.

Pamela Humphrey, who writes as Remi Carrington, also releases books under her own name. Visit PhreyPress.com for more information about her books.

ABOUT THE AUTHOR

Remi Carrington is a figment of Pamela Humphrey's imagination. She loves romance & chocolate, enjoys disappearing into a delicious book, and considers people-watching a sport. She was born in the pages of the novel *Just You* and then grew into an alter ego.

She writes sweet romance set in Texas. Her books are part of the Phrey Press imprint.

facebook.com/remiromance
twitter.com/phreypress
instagram.com/phreypress

Made in the USA
Coppell, TX
04 September 2023